A

WILLS CREEK

Christmas

A
WILLS CREEK
Christmas

A COLLECTION OF FICTIONAL
FEEL-GOOD SHORT STORIES ABOUT CHRISTMAS,
BY THE CAMBRIDGE WRITERS WORKSHOP

RAINY DAY PUBLISHING
CAMBRIDGE, OHIO

ABOUT THE COVER

When AVC Communications throws the switch on the 2010 Guernsey County Courthouse holiday lights and music show, onlookers will witness seasonal illumination amplified to a scale never before seen in the local area. The historic centerpiece of downtown Cambridge comes alive with thousands of colorful lights, synchronized to both traditional and contemporary holiday music.

The courthouse lends its magnificent 1881 design to an intricately-choreographed 21st Century eyefest, including more than 26,000 lights, 15,000 of which outline the structure's unique architectural details. Thirty-nine animated displays complete the holiday spectacle.

AVC designed the 2010 display, creating four different 12-minute shows that play through the holiday season. Each presentation makes use of more than 430 electrical circuits, each computer controlled in tenth-of-a-second increments and painstakingly synchronized to a holiday soundtrack. There is new music, including contemporary and kids' favorites, and new, animated lights for the 2010 season. (Cover photos by Michael Neilson, *Daily Jeffersonian*, and Ryan Pavlov.)

A Wills Creek Christmas
ISBN 978-0-615-40752-4

RAINY DAY PUBLISHING
CAMBRIDGE, OHIO

CONTENTS

PREFACE

A Wills Creek Christmas is the fourth book published by the Cambridge Writers Workshop in three years. Earlier works include *The Day We Learned To Write & Other Acts of Madness*, *The Wills Creek Chronicles*, and *The Wills Creek Trilogies*. CWW tries to entertain readers with short fictional stories set against the Wills Creek backdrop.

Special thanks to the Crossroads Branch Library and Christ United Methodist Church for providing our meeting rooms. We wish also to acknowledge *The Daily and Sunday Jeffersonian*, AVC Communications, *Jeffersonian* photographers Mike Neilson and Ryan Pavlov, and the Cambridge/Guernsey County Visitors and Convention Bureau. We also appreciate the hard work put into this book by Aaron Keirns of Little River Publishing, who designed this book.

We enjoyed writing these stories and willingly acknowledge that any misspellings or grammatical errors are our own.

Jerry Wolfrom
Coordinator

MISSION STATEMENT

The Cambridge Writers Workshop is an unofficial, not-for-profit organization established to provide an environment designed to educate local writers, encourage them to continue writing, expand their literary horizons and enhance their creative abilities in order to broaden their future choices in the publication of their own works.

FOREWORD

My heart beat violently as I opened and read the contents of the letter. It stated that I was appointed to Wills Creek circuit, to travel alone." Thus begins the account by Reverend James B. Finley of his 1809 assignment to travel the roots and branches of the Wills Creek territory as a solo circuit-riding Methodist Episcopal minister. Coming from the somewhat more settled Cincinnati area, he had great hesitation about bringing his family into the wilderness then being settled along Zane's recent trace.

Alone at first, the young preacher built himself a cabin somewhere near present day Lore City, then sent for his wife and child to join him. Near Christmas 1809, after four months apart, a joyous family reunion took place along Wills Creek's Leatherwood branch, a few miles southeast of Cambridge. This is one of the earliest accounts both of Christian ministry and of events of the Christmas season in Guernsey County.

Though Christianity had been introduced to the general Guernsey County area in the 1770's by Moravian missionaries building settlements in neighboring Tuscarawas County, it may not have been until Zane's Trace came through in 1798 that Christmas itself was significantly celebrated in the county, perhaps by a Wills Creek ferry keeper whose name we no longer are sure of. Five years later, in 1803, Ohio became a state at about the same time that a bridge "came" to Cambridge (pun intended), courtesy of the legislature of the Northwest Territory. Cambridge itself wasn't officially platted into existence until three years later, in 1806, its founding having had a lot to do with the bridge.

The aforementioned 470-mile Methodist Episcopal Wills Creek preaching circuit, servicing Cambridge, Barnesville, Morristown, New Philadelphia, Canton, and Zanesville, was established somewhat before 1809 by a Reverend James Watts. It took a month to ride the circuit, but the hardy preachers of that day did it to spread the gospel, no doubt even in many a cold and snowy winter season.

Half a century later, by the first year of the Civil War, sparse microfilmed newspaper records show two Methodist churches, two Presbyterian, and one Baptist church in Cambridge in steady operation. Shortly before that Christmas of 1861, a "rascal" broke a grocery store window to steal a few Christmas toys. But that news was more than counterbalanced by a call to service to the citizens of Cambridge, printed in the same newspaper edition, to make sure the family of every local soldier gone off to war had a splendid Christmas dinner at their table.

When war's end came in 1865, the Christmas ads took a lighthearted turn: "Parents can procure nice presents at McKissons' for their children, young gentlemen for their sisters; and if they have no sisters they can buy presents for somebody else's sister, which perhaps most of them would prefer doing."

Moving onward, at the turn of the year 2000, I found a familiar name in searching through newspaper archives from Christmas a hundred years earlier. Back then, for a celebration at the United Presbyterian Church, "Music was furnished by Miss Estella McCartney..." Fifty-eight years later, when I returned to Cambridge to practice law, the same, elderly Miss McCartney rented a portion of her home to me as my office. When she died in the mid-1960's, I purchased the building and have practiced there to this day, 52 years in her old home. It's an unusual feeling when a century of history catches up with you like that, as if one is almost joining in with history, albeit the pleasant history of Christmas 1899.

Then, in 1938, when I was nine years old, a Christmas decoration contest was run in the Cambridge area. My father's boss, Joe Aker, designed a motorized, animated display for his front porch, featuring Santa, one reindeer, a dog, a doll, and a hitchhiking moon. It didn't win the contest, but the homegrown display continued to grow year after year. When *Rudolph the Red-Nosed Reindeer* became a hit song in the late 1940's, the reindeer accommodatingly began sporting a red light bulb nose. A bear, a seal, a rabbit, and an elf joined the Christmas porch parade too.

Joe Aker's old porch display was an enjoyable annual Cambridge Christmas constant for many a year. When my children came along, I took them to see it too. Then, in 1968, after Joe Aker retired and moved away, I took over the display and have kept that old friend from 1938 running on the house porch for the past 42 consecutive

Christmases, with more intended to come.

Should you happen by North Tenth Street during the Christmas season, last house on the left before the City Park, feel free to stop by for a visit and a gander at the old, working front porch memory of a simpler time, of Christmas 1938. And perhaps think also of the young Estella McCartney playing holiday piano in 1899, or of the meals once served in Cambridge for the kin of Union soldiers, or a family Christmastime reunion in a long lost, little log cabin out on Leatherwood more than two hundred years ago.

There's a long and sometimes touching history of Christmases along the Wills Creek valley. May the memory of those Christmases past add to your enjoyment of the stories in this book. And, by the way, Merry Christmas.

Russell H. Booth, Jr.

EARLY CHURCHES IN GUERNSEY COUNTY

Christmas has been an important part of life in Guernsey County for more than 150 years, when newcomers to the area created a blend of traditions from many different countries. Since then, Christmas is observed here as an important celebration of peace and tranquility.

OLD CONCORD UNITED METHODIST CHURCH

The Old Concord United Methodist Church, located about two miles east of Senecaville on Seneca Lake was founded in 1859. It is primarily used today as a vacation ministry to campers and tourists who visit the lake. The church has been in continuous operation for over 150 years.

OLD SALEM BAPTIST CHURCH

The Old Salem Baptist Church is located in a peaceful, picturesque setting on a hill just off Salem Road, four miles east of Lore City. Regular Sunday services are still conducted there. Headstones in the adjacent cemetery date back to the early 1800's.

ST. PATRICK'S CATHOLIC CHURCH

Originally built in Old Washington, St. Patrick's Catholic Church was later moved to its present site at Gibson Station. Details on the church are vague, but it is believed that it was built in the early 1850's.

CAMBRIDGE'S DICKENS VICTORIAN VILLAGE

SEE PAGES 51—58

Charles Dickens would feel at home strolling through the 1800's Dickens Victorian Village in Cambridge, Ohio. The Christmas event runs November 1, 2010 through January 8, 2011.

Seventy-four Dickens-era scenes, stationed beside forty historic lampposts and benches, line Wheeling Avenue from Sixth to Eleventh Streets. Nearly 150 life-sized figures welcome visitors to the 1800's. From realistic ladies and gentlemen taking daily constitutionals on the courthouse lawn to period characters in first and second story windows, downtown Cambridge comes alive with history. Horse-drawn carriages highlight the ambiance.

Visitors are welcome to take tea in The SweeTea Tea Boutique on designated Saturdays during the ten-week event. Or imbibe specialty drinks in local pubs during an old-fashioned pub-crawl. Join the Great Expectations Chocolate Walk for tantalizing chocolate treats.

Stop to visit costumed volunteers at Ye Ole Curiosity Shoppe and Dickens Welcome Center with Imagination Station. Have pictures taken in period costume; purchase Dickens and holiday souvenirs; roam Rotary Square, a small Victorian Village modeled after shops from Charles Dickens' stories. During Peddler Weekends, buy the wares of heritage artisans dressed in 1800's attire.

Enjoy the Steeple Walk, viewing varied architectural styles of select area churches. Dance at the Fezziwig Ball, attend concerts, and marvel at gingerbread dwellings. Dazzle your senses with the Guernsey County Courthouse Holiday Music and Light Show.

Yes, Charles Dickens would feel right at home in the Dickens Victorian Village, just a short stroll from historic Wills Creek.

– MARILYN DURR

BEVERLY WENCEK KERR

Icy Road Home

Ping! Ping! Ice hit against the windshield. Black ice covered the road! Semi trucks skidded and cars went off the road, crashing into each other like a demolition derby. Being almost dark, danger seemed all around. Quickly finding a place to stop seemed the answer. Maryann enjoyed driving across the country on the back roads but always stopped when the weather got bad to avoid playing bumper cars on the highway.

Off to the side, she saw a motel sign blinking in the early evening hours. Her prayers had been answered! After slowly driving into the parking lot, she carefully walked across the slippery blacktop and opened the office door.

Sitting by an old wood burner was a jolly bearded man dressed in bib overalls, plaid shirt, and a friendly smile. He slowly got up from his rocker when he heard the door open. This easy-going man reminded her of Uncle Jake, who lived in a cabin along Wills Creek back home.

Maryann quickly asked, "Do you have a room for the night? That road reminds me of an ice skating rink."

"Of course I have an extra room," said the friendly man, "but I don't take credit cards. It will have to be cash."

Traveling alone, Maryann didn't have a lot of cash with her. But if she could have a place to stay tonight, Maryann would give him her last nickel.

Pleasantly, the bearded man said, "A room will be $35. Leave the key on the dresser in the morning." That seemed more than reasonable, especially tonight.

This absolutely charming room felt safe, being located next door to the office. With a quilted flowered bedspread and stained glass lamp for reading, the room gave you the feeling of home. Without TV in the room, she would go to sleep reading one of the books she always brought with her.

Maryann felt thankful to be out of the storm, as she was headed home for Christmas with her family. Her sons lived in the small town of Kimbolton on the edge of Wills Creek. She drifted to sleep with thoughts of the Christmas tree and dinner down the road a few hundred miles.

In the morning, she awoke to find the ice melted by the warm morning sun. After checking the road atlas, it appeared she would be in Cambridge in about eight hours. But first it would be fun to stop at a local restaurant for a cup of coffee and a sweet roll. Restaurants in small towns always provided interesting stories about the area.

Everyone in this small town seemed surprised to see a stranger in their midst. Maryann told them that she was headed back to Ohio for the holidays and, when that ice storm hit, breathed a sigh of relief to see their little motel along the way.

They looked at each other with quizzical looks on their faces and asked, "Motel? We don't have a motel here."

Maryann laughed and said, "Why, the one down on the corner where the road comes off to your town."

They exclaimed, rolling their eyes, "That motel hasn't been open for ten years!"

Now Maryann felt quite confused. She knew she had spent the night down on the corner. Diners in the restaurant shook their heads, thinking this stranger acted like a confused old lady. So Maryann went back and checked out the corner where she rested from the storm. She drove to the end of the road and saw what looked like a former motel, but there was no sign and there was no one there—no cars, no manager, no signs of an open motel!

Thrills ran down her spine as she realized her angels accompanied her again and provided a safe place during the storm. Never knew that angels wore bib overalls!

SAMUEL D. BESKET

YES, ERIC,
THERE IS A SANTA CLAUS

Eric, time to get up. Breakfast is ready. I'm not going to call you again,... Eric!"

Curled up in a ball, Eric didn't want to get up. It was Saturday and he wanted to sleep in. Tomorrow he would have to get up early for church.

"Eric, don't make me come up there. Get out of bed right now. I have some errands for you to run, and it snowed last night. Our sidewalks and Mr. Keiner's need shoveled."

Grumbling as he plodded down the stairs, Eric wasn't in a good mood. It was bad enough he had to shovel their walk, but why did he have to do Mr. Keiner's? As he pulled his chair up to the table, his mom placed three large pancakes on his plate.

"Eat up, lunch will be late today. We have a lot of chores to do this morning before we go to town."

"Mom, I don't like Mr. Keiner. He is old and grumpy. Why do I have to shovel his walk? I liked Mrs. Keiner; she always baked cookies for me."

"Mrs. Keiner is baking cookies for the angels now, so we have to be nice to Mr. Keiner. Stop grinding on this and eat. We'll go to town as soon as you're done with the sidewalks."

Opening the gate to Mr. Keiner's yard, Eric shoveled a path to the front door, then around back to the outhouse. Looking up, he saw Mr.Keiner watching him through the window. As he walked around the house, he heard the front door open. Mr. Keiner stepped out on the porch. Handing an empty plate to Eric, he said, "Tell your mom thanks for the pie. It was delicious." Nodding, Eric grabbed the plate as he headed for home.

Later, while his mom grocery shopped at Stan's Red and White Store, Eric went next door to Wills Creek Hardware. Looking into the window, he smiled. It was still there, a bright red and blue Lightning Glider sled. He closed his eyes, dreaming of flying down Christopher's Hill. His mom's voice broke into his daydreaming.

"Eric, time to go. We need to get home so I can bake cookies for the church Christmas play tonight."

"Come here, Mom. I want to show you something."

"I know what you want to show me, but we can't afford that sled right now. It's been a hard year, with your father losing his job and all."

"How about Santa? I wrote him a letter. Maybe he could bring me one?"

Stopping and looking into Eric's eyes, his mother told him, "Santa is for little kids. You're a big boy now. Maybe next year."

Soon it was Christmas Eve. Eric couldn't help think of the sled at the hardware store. Walking with his parents to candlelight service that evening, they passed the darkened hardware store. Eric's eyes lit up when he saw that the sled was gone from the window. He was on his best behavior during the service. Later that evening as he lay in bed, his hopes were high. He drifted off to sleep dreaming of the new sled.

Early Christmas morning, Eric raced down the stairs, only to have his hopes dashed when there wasn't a sled under the tree. Sadly, he opened gifts containing socks, shirts, and underwear.

"Eric, I want you to take a plate of food to Mr. Keiner," his mom said. "He is all alone on Christmas Day."

Opening the door, Eric shouted as he dropped the plate of food. There, leaning on the porch railing, was a shiny new Lightning Glider. Hearing the commotion, his mother ran to look. "Look, Mom, there is a Santa Claus. See, I told you; he got my letter."

As she bent down to pick up the broken plate, his mother saw a fresh set of footprints in the snow going to and from Mr. Keiner's house. Turning to her son, she shouted, "Yes Eric, there is a Santa Claus."

But by that time Eric was out of earshot, gliding down the hill on his shiny new sled.

JOY L. WILBERT ERSKINE

Jingles' New Job

Christmas at Kate's house is always a luminous affair. Preparations begin the moment the dishes are cleared away from Thanksgiving dinner. No holiday tradition goes uncelebrated. No act of kindness goes undone. Every detail is lovingly carried out. Kate radiates a welcoming glow throughout the year, but Christmas always brings out the extraordinary in our daughter.

You'd never guess now that Kate was once at rock bottom. Addiction directed her path down a road that no one would otherwise choose to follow. It was hard on us all. We thought we'd never see the real Kate again, that she'd been taken from us forever.

That was before Jingles, a tri-color basset hound. He turned up on our back porch on the outskirts of Cambridge on a snowy Friday night. He looked like he'd fallen into Wills Creek. A weaker, colder, more emaciated, desperate pup you never saw. I caught him nosing around the trash bin, trying to knock it over. The tantalizing aroma of beef scraps tormented him. It was sad to watch his struggle to topple the bin. Kate had just put the dishes in the dishwasher, turning it on as I peeked out the door window. "Jim, come look at this," I called to my husband.

Kate sidled up behind us, glancing momentarily over our shoulders. "It's just a stupid dog," she mumbled.

Assessing the situation, Jim said, "I'll get my work gloves from the basement. Round up something for the poor animal to eat, Kate."

She flashed him a hateful look, but opened the refrigerator. "Stupid dog," she growled under her breath.

It was Christmas and Kate was on house arrest. Her probation officer took a tougher stance after her last brush with the law. She wore an ankle monitor and had to report in every day. "I don't care if you hate me for this now," he'd said. "Down the road, you'll thank me." Kate did hate her probation officer, but she despised me and her dad. She might as well have been an angry bear shackled to a post by a trap.

"You don't even *want* to help me," she accused venomously. "I hate you!" But she was beyond our help.

Work gloves found, Jim returned to the kitchen. Kate had unwrapped the few slices of beef left over from dinner. "Thanks, Kate," he smiled. "Let's see if this dog is too hungry to be friendly."

He edged the door open slowly. "Nice dog. Are you hungry, fella? Looks like things've been a little rocky for you lately."

Jim tossed a bite of beef to the basset. The dog seemed to gulp back a grateful sob, then quickly choked the meat down. Jim threw another bite, then another. Soon he was hand-feeding the poor lost pooch. When the meat was gone, we set out water and brought out an old blanket. He drank deeply. As I wrapped the blanket around him and scratched his ears, he slumped to the ground in exhaustion.

The next morning, the dog was still there when Kate carried her cereal out to the picnic table, her usual practice, winter or summer. "What're you still doing here?" she grumped.

He just lay still, looking her over as if sizing her up. With a huff, Kate parked unceremoniously on the bench. "Stupid dog," she muttered, dipping her spoon into the bowl. Slowly, the dog crept forward. Watching out of the corner of her eye, Kate accused, "Don't think you're gonna get my breakfast, mutt."

Closer and closer he wriggled until, with a contented sigh, he plopped onto Kate's slippered feet. Much later, Kate told us she named him 'Jingles' because he somehow rang a little bell in her soul that day. "I kinda related to his situation." That was the day our Kate started home.

This Christmas, Kate is radiant as she passes the cranberries to my dear son-in-law. I offer a silent, grateful prayer that Jingles found us that cold December years ago. Now both are healthy and he's a beloved member of the family. Jingles' job now is simply enduring the tugs and thumps of our darling granddaughter, Temperance Noelle, born one year ago today. She's a lucky little girl. She inherited her mother's smile.

JERRY WOLFROM

A PRAYER FOR DANNY

For years, the Stonek family had gathered at the old home place on Christmas Eve. Tomas and his wife, Lenka, loved hosting their seven grown children and twenty-one grandchildren. It was the only time when everyone in the family gathered under one roof.

Tomas, a retired miner, had spent thirty years at backbreaking pick and shovel work in underground mines. The large two-story white frame house, on a hill just south of Byesville above Wills Creek, had been a boarding house for miners in 1901. At Christmastime, Lenka placed candles in each of the twenty windows; the Christmas tree in the sprawling living room was the largest, most brightly decorated tree around.

But disturbing news came five days before Christmas of 1950. A short telegram from the War Department advised the family that their son, Daniel, had been seriously wounded in action near the Yalu River, South Korea. There was no other information.

The Stonek's were proud of their patriotism and military record. Fourteen Stonek's had served in the Spanish-American War, World War I, and World War II. Danny's older brothers, Evan and Jim, were decorated Marines in World War II. Danny, just turned 19, was trained as a Marine combat engineer and sent to Korea after eight weeks of basic training.

The news stunned the Stonek's, who spent the next several days in subdued agony. Lenka made sure the little banner trimmed in gold with the blue star in the middle was prominently displayed on the front door to honor her youngest son, the fun-loving jokester of the family. She prayed she wouldn't have to replace that blue star with a gold one.

Despite their deep anguish, Tomas and Lenka decided the family Christmas gathering would go on as planned. At noon on Christmas Eve, a soft snow enveloped the Wills Valley, continuing to accumulate until dark. It was a perfect Christmas backdrop that would have brought joy to the family under ordinary circumstances.

Tomas hid his sadness by digging out ten old but workable strings of colored lights and draping them on outside pine trees. Now the entire Stonek home was ablaze in a festive glow. Lenka put the finishing touches on two plump turkeys, along with a dozen side dishes and mouth-watering Czech pastries.

Tomas built a roaring fire in the stone fireplace anchoring one end of the living room. The couple was determined to make it a pleasant event despite not knowing the whereabouts of one badly injured family member in a land thousands of miles away. Danny, in a letter several weeks earlier, began with, "Greetings from the land of the Frozen Chosen." Enclosed were several pictures of himself dressed like an Eskimo and covered with snow.

The families began arriving at six with some weak "Merry Christmas" greetings. Tomas and Lenka put on their best happy faces, but the children noticed that both quivered when hugged.

Everyone worked to keep the dinner lighthearted, but the joyous spirit of past Christmases didn't come through. No one was surprised when Tomas asked for a special prayer for Danny, during which he broke down completely. Lenka too totally lost her composure.

Finally, Tomas said, "Okay, this is Christmas....everyone gather around the tree to see if Santa left anything." Squealing with delight, the bright-eyed grandchildren raced for the living room. Evan would pass out the gifts. Paper and ribbons flew in all directions.

Then came a loud banging on the front door, followed by a voice thundering, "Hey! Is this the Stonek house? ...Any chance a hungry soldier could get a turkey leg to chew on around here?"

After several seconds of shocked silence, all thirty Stonek voices screamed and cried out, "Danny!" Just inside the front door stood the youthful soldier in full uniform. Smiling broadly, he hobbled into the living room on crutches, dragging a cast from ankle to hip on his left leg.

With that familiar impish grin, Danny said, "Tried to get here earlier but the roads from Columbus were a mess."

Tomas, tears of joy running down his flushed cheeks, could only murmur, "But....how...?"

Danny smiled. "Caught a last-minute Army transport out of Seoul yesterday. Been trying to get here from San Francisco all day. Any oyster dressing left?"

HARRIETTE ORR

CHRISTMAS WITH A BANG

It is noon on Christmas day. The Banning family has gathered at the old farm up over the hill from Wills Creek and down the road a piece on Route 40.

There are nine siblings, their spouses, and many, many children. Grandpa has asked the blessing and everyone sang "Old Hundred." Our numbers are so great that we have to eat in shifts. A second table has been brought into the large kitchen, with chairs borrowed from the McCracken Funeral Home.

Bertie has been busy all week preparing food. Chickens were butchered and hams were baked. Noodles, mashed potatoes and gravy, sweet potatoes, oyster dressing, coleslaw, green beans, and succotash are ready to be served. Dozens of beautiful rolls are waiting to be slathered with home-churned butter and jams. Huge kettles are simmering on the stove. Cakes, pies, cookies, and fruitcake are ready for dessert.

The men eat first. The women serve the food and take away the plates to be washed and used again. The little kids keep watch by peeking around the corner, hoping there is going to be enough food left for them, and wishing the men would hurry up.

Finally, the men head out of the kitchen. The women and kids reset the table. As they get ready to pass the food, there stands Grandpa Banning in the kitchen doorway with a rifle. Bertie, terrified of guns, yells, "Dad, what on earth are you doing getting that gun out with all these people here?"

Grandpa says, "Now, you just never mind. William here wants to see my gun. It's not loaded."

About that time the gun goes off—BANG! It shoots a hole clean through the floor, scaring everyone to death.

A family of mice that had been hiding under the bookcase comes running out. Uncle Al steps on one, smashing it dead. The others run into the kitchen.

The women scatter, with Bertie climbing up on her chair and screaming every time a mouse comes near.

Someone brings in one of the barn cats and puts her down, thinking she will catch the mice. Instead she runs and hides.

Grandpa lets his dog, Ol' Sport, into the house. Ol' Sport is known to be "the best ratter in Guernsey County." The chase is on. The cat is scared of the dog and runs up the curtains. "Get that cat out of here," sputters Bertie.

Bob gets the broom to swat the mice. Both he and the yelping dog run around the kitchen. Whenever they get near Bertie, she lets out a blood-curdling scream. Up the leg of her chair scurries a mouse. Standing on the seat of the chair, Bertie grabs the chair back, which lets go, causing her to fall face-down into the mashed potatoes. What a mess!!

A mouse races into the sitting room, with Bob and the dog in hot pursuit. Under the couch goes the mouse. Now the dog is barking and Bob is poking under the couch with the broom. Finally the mouse runs out. Ol' Sport corners it. The dog, a spaniel mix, has long ears. The mouse grabs the outside of Ol' Sport's ear and hangs on. The dog tries franticly to get the mouse off his ear by running in circles, trying to bite it. Bob takes the broom and hits the dog on the head, knocking the mouse to the floor. Uncle Al steps up and squashes it dead. Grandpa picks it up by the tail and throws it out to the cats.

All the while, Bertie is crying, sputtering mashed potatoes, and cursing that worthless cat. They finally calm her down and clean her up. The dog is okay, but still looking for a mouse. As soon as the door opens, the cat makes a mad dash for freedom.

This has been the most exciting Christmas dinner our family ever had, and the only one that started off with such a bang.

PAM RITCHEY

THE FORGOTTEN STAR

The trip home for Christmas wasn't going as smoothly as I'd hoped. First was a flat tire, now the coney dog from that greasy spoon where we ate lunch wasn't agreeing with me. And we still had 200 miles to go!

Much to my relief, the sickness didn't last long, and the remainder of our trip back to Kimbolton was uneventful. I couldn't wait to see my parents and brothers and sisters. Including all the grandkids, there were 23 of us. As the oldest, it was up to me to plan family gatherings. This was the first time I was able to get everyone together to celebrate Christmas in years.

Sitting on a hill above Wills Creek, the beautiful old two-story farmhouse brought back memories of childhood. Swinging on the rope hanging from the old oak tree, sliding down the curved banister, the cupola lighting the attic…

The cupola in the attic! That's where I saw the star!

I must have been around 17 years old when the beautiful silver star that always adorned the top of our Christmas tree disappeared. It was a wondrous thing, so sparkly and bright that it seemed to glow with God's grace. No one knew what happened to it. One year it was just gone. An angel took its place and over time the star was forgotten.

"Tammy, do you remember the star that we used to put on the tree?" I asked my sister while we were unpacking. At 26, she was the youngest of my four siblings.

"Huh? Oh, that old thing…vaguely. Why do you ask?" she replied.

"I was thinking about it on the way here. I can remember seeing it in the attic. Don't know when it was, but I'd like to go look. Want to join me?"

Tammy declined my invitation. The attic used to be her favorite place to play. She must have outgrown it when she was around ten though, and didn't like it after that. I found our brother, Jeremiah, and talked him into tagging along.

In the dusty attic, steamer trunks, old tables, and cardboard boxes full of forgotten treasure created a maze-like pathway. The small wainscoting door to the cupola stood behind years of cobwebs.

Either I grew a lot or that door shrunk, because it was much smaller than I remembered. Wiping away the cobwebs with an old duster, I had to crouch to enter the room. Waist high shelves occupied by various small boxes lined the walls and were topped by rows of shuttered windows. Dolls, wooden blocks, crayons, and a couple plastic horses lie on the floor, covered with dust.

Jeremiah and I started at opposite sides of the door in the octagonal room, looking through boxes for any sign of the star. Buried under a stack of Tammy's fifth grade papers, I found a single silver point. The star was broken.

My dear brother refused to give up. He continued rummaging through boxes until he found our beautiful star's remaining portion.

"How did it get broken?" I asked Jeremiah.

"I don't know. I barely remember it, but I bet I can fix it," he replied.

As children, we followed the family tradition of decorating the tree on the day before Christmas Eve. This year, Mom and Dad waited until the last of us were home to begin the festivities.

While Dad and my brother, Scot, went out to pick the right tree, the rest of us gathered up the decorations. Boxes and bags were pulled out of closets and piled in the living room awaiting their return.

"Mom, do you know what happened to the star?" I said.

"No. I wish I did though. That star peered down from the top of my mother's tree. It's long gone now," she said as she took the angel from its box.

Tammy started sobbing and said, "I'm so sorry, Mama. I was looking at it and it broke. I hid it in the attic."

"It's not broken now," said Jeremiah, taking it from behind him.

The look of amazement and thankfulness in our mother's eyes when her family treasure was returned was the best present a person could wish for.

DICK METHENEY

HOME FOR THE HOLIDAYS

Our father worked at RCA for years and now the plant was closed. The products made in our local factories were being made cheaper in foreign countries. Dad and Mom had stayed up late into the night talking about what he should do. The very next morning, Dad packed his clothes into a ratty old suitcase and tossed it in the back of his ten-year-old Chevy.

He hugged and kissed us all and drove off down the gravel road. Mom said he was going north to try to find work. That was not at all unusual; most of our neighbors had already left Guernsey County for the north.

Dad tried the steel mills in Massillon and Canton, Akron's rubber factories, and Cleveland's auto factories and steel mills with no luck. He finally got hired at the Lorain Ford Assembly Plant at Lorain, Ohio.

Dad had written to Mom, telling her he was going to try to come home for Christmas if he could get the time off. We were excited because Dad had not been home since he had gone north six weeks earlier.

Ten days before Christmas, my younger brother, George, and I took Dad's ax and climbed the steep hill behind our house. After some serious consultation, we cut down a white pine about seven feet tall. It was tough work for the two of us to drag it down the hillside to the house.

With more than a little help from Mom we got it set up in the living room. The younger kids made colored paper chains, cutting star and snowflake shapes out of aluminum foil for decorations. George and I strung popcorn on a string to make long strands to drape over the tree.

Our little country church always has a brief service on Christmas Eve. As Mom and the five of us kids walked down the gravel road toward the church, snow began to fall. We were joined by more and more of our neighbors as we trudged through the cold winter evening. Someone mentioned the radio had predicted twelve inches of snow by morning.

This news brought a worried look to Mom's face. That old Chevy, with its bald tires and worn-out engine, would be dangerous on such a long journey in that much snow. When I caught a glimpse of George's face, I could see he had his mouth clamped shut in a concerted effort to hold back his tears. I realized my lips were pressed tightly closed too.

The church service was brief, just a few songs and a little skit put on by the five- and six-year-olds. There was Kool-Aid and cookies for the kids and coffee for the adults. Each kid got a candy cane and a tiny ornament for their tree. The preacher said an extra long prayer for family members who were traveling on this stormy night. We hurried toward home in the snowy darkness.

Before she went upstairs to put the younger kids to bed, Mom told George to bring in enough wood for the night. I was to shake the ashes down and load both the stove in the living room and the cookstove in the kitchen. That was unusual because normally we let the fire in the cookstove go out overnight to save on wood.

Mom sent George and me up to bed, saying, "I'm not very sleepy yet. I'm going to stay up and do some baking while you kids are in bed."

George and I went up to bed, but we both knew she was waiting up for Dad to come home. Just as I was dropping off to sleep, I could hear George start to sob. I left my bed and sat on the edge of his with one hand patting his shoulder until he finally fell asleep.

It was broad daylight when I woke up. I got out of bed and looked out the window to see how much it snowed. To my delight, I saw that ratty old green Chevy sitting in our driveway. Dad had made it home for Christmas after all.

DONA McCONNELL

FAMILY TROUBLES

The elderly couple struggled up the stairs and down the hall, gazing at the row of doors. The man's large frame was covered by a black trench coat and topped by a toboggan pulled tightly over his head. Black boots stuck out below the coat.

The woman sported a leopard faux fur cape and matching hat. Wisps of blonde bangs were visible below the hat and above cat-eye glasses studded with rhinestones. "Here it is," the woman said. The stencil on the door read, "Christine Bunchen, Marriage Counseling."

Gingerly, the couple entered the reception room.

"Mr. and Mrs. Clausen?" the receptionist inquired. "The doctor is waiting. Please go in."

The doctor positioned the couple in two large chairs and sat directly facing them, notebook at the ready.

"Let's start with a brief description of your problems. Mr. Clausen, why don't you start? And please, make yourself comfortable."

The man opened the coat to reveal a bright red suit, trimmed in white fur. His hair was snow white, as well. The therapist gasped.

"You can see why we don't use our real names," the man said. "People don't expect to see Santa Claus in October."

"That's why we never go out," the woman grumbled. "How would you like staying at home eleven months of the year?" she asked the therapist.

"You do have something of an unusual situation, Mrs., uh, Claus?"

"You're not sure, right? Because I don't have white hair? My hair used to be blonde!" Mrs. Claus countered angrily, ignoring the doctor. "He made me start bleaching it when I was 25!"

Her husband interrupted before the therapist could speak.

"People want Mrs. Claus. Not a Marilyn Monroe look-alike."

The therapist dove into the gap in the conversation. "It's, uh, clear that you have an unusual situation. I think …."

"He's a total control freak," the woman said to the therapist.

"I have to be in control," Santa answered angrily. "The elves and I have only 363 days to make toys for every child in the world. And just one day to pack them on the sled."

"Don't tell me how many days there are," his wife answered. "That's how many days I cook for those hungry mini-maniacs!"

"They're four-foot-two," the man said. "How much can they eat?"

"A lot, considering there are 278 of them!"

"It takes elves to make toys. With all those remakes of 'The Wizard of Oz' lately, they're all leaving the North Pole to play Munchkins on Broadway!"

"Do you realize I've been wearing the same dress for over a century?" Mrs. Claus continued, ignoring her husband. "And red isn't even on my color wheel. I need my own look."

"You've got a look alright," Santa replied. "You look like a cheetah fell out of a tree onto your head and shoulders."

"Me?" Mrs. Claus countered. "What woman wants a man with a stomach that shakes like a bowl full of jelly?" She looked at Dr. Bunchen for understanding, but Mr. Claus had grabbed the conversation like a football and was headed downfield.

"I don't have a choice. I have to eat the cookies the kids leave for me."

"You might want to remember there are 365 nights, too," Mrs. Claus commented sarcastically.

"How did you two meet?" the doctor asked, trying to deflect the hostility. "If nobody believes Santa is real…"

"How do you think it feels to be an 'imaginary' person?" Santa's countenance took on a sad look.

"There, there," Mrs. Claus said softly. "The little kids think you're real. The elves believe. And, of course, I know you're real."

"What would I do without you?" Santa patted his wife's hand. The two exchanged a warm glance. "Actually, I kind of like your new look," Santa said.

Mrs. Claus glowed. "You do?"

"Let's go home," Santa said warmly.

The couple rose and, hand in hand, quickly exited the room.

"But, we're just getting started," the counselor said to the empty space.

She stood and let out a deep sigh. "And to all a good night," she said softly.

BARBARA KERNODLE-ALLEN

MARY ANN'S FIRST JOB

Disillusioned with love, recently divorced, Mary Ann moved back to the old hometown. Raising her toddler near family, who could be counted on for babysitting and emotional support, was a primary consideration.

Mary Ann leased an apartment along Wills Creek Valley Drive and began a search for steady employment with disappointing results. The only job available was part-time for the Christmas holidays at Doan's Department Store in the heart of downtown Cambridge. The pay was barely enough to cover necessities, but with few skills and no experience, she was lucky to find it. Mary Ann spent many sleepless nights worrying about finances. Her meager savings wouldn't last long. "What am I going to do after Christmas?"

Learning to use the old-fashioned pneumatic tubes to send money and sales slips back to the store office was as much a challenge as dealing with customers. Office manager, Jim, could be heard calling Mary Ann's name when she put the cartridge in upside down or forgot to include the sales slip. Jim had little patience for mistakes.

As Christmas drew near, confidence grew and errors decreased. Jim only called out to Mary Ann once or twice a day. She began to like waiting on customers, and restocking the jewelry counter became a favorite task. Store manager, Mr. Shively, mentioned, "There might be a full-time opening after Christmas, but the other part-time clerk wants it, too." Mary Ann realized she didn't have much chance of getting it. The other clerk had more experience and made fewer mistakes.

Ten minutes till closing time on the last day before the holiday, a young man, poorly dressed in dirty work clothes, rushed up to the jewelry counter. "I just got paid. I need a gift for my wife."

As he browsed through the necklaces, pins, bracelets, and earrings, he told Mary Ann his new bride loved jewelry. He talked about her sweetness, her patience, and her prettiness while he looked at piece after piece of high priced crystals and sets of Trifari. Each time he asked, "How much is this?" disappointment flooded his face as he put it back on the counter. Head down, shoulders slumped, he started to walk away.

Mary Ann called him back. "Wait, I have an idea. Do you have enough for one of these jewelry boxes?"

"Yeah, but what good is a box with nothin' to put in it?"

"Why don't you give her a pretty jewelry box with a promise to fill it a little every Christmas till it's full? You could write the promise on a card and put that in the box this year."

Mary Ann picked up a pretty ivory box trimmed in gold. Opening it to display the red velvet lining caused the musical box to play a tinkling rendition of "Lara's Theme" from *Dr. Zhivago*. Her young customer grinned as he handed over his money in small bills and change.

The closing bell rang just as the cartridge was sucked into the tube. The pneumatic system shut off with the cartridge, sales slip, and the last of the man's money stuck somewhere between the jewelry department and the store's business office.

"Mary Ann!" Jim called. "What did you do now? We can't get the cartridge out till the store opens."

Clerk and customer stared at each other in dismay.

"Wait. I think I can fix this."

Mary Ann reached under the counter, grabbed her purse, and rushed back to the office window.

"I can pay for it and you can reimburse me when the store opens after Christmas. Please, Jim. It's all the money he has."

Jim frowned and grumbled, "Well, alright. It's going to mess up my bookwork, but okay."

Mr. Shively caught Mary Ann when she clocked out that night.

"I heard what happened. You caused a problem, then solved it with a generous act. That full-time job is yours after Christmas. Have a Merry Christmas."

Hugging her little one that night, Mary Ann whispered, "Mommy got the job. Everything's going to be fine."

JOETTA VARANASI

FAMILY KEEPS HOLIDAY TRADITION

The National Weather Center in Pittsburgh called for a blizzard. Southeastern Ohio was preparing for the worst. Stores were busy with last-minute Christmas shoppers buying supplies for the predicted storm.

Grandpa Dominick and Grandma Cecilia Bruno had eight children and 20 grandchildren. Their extended families would join them as usual for Christmas Eve dinner.

The day before Christmas Eve, the women were working on the traditional Christmas Eve dinner. The smell of Italian nut rolls baking in the oven penetrated through the house. Dean Martin was singing "Home for the Holidays." Preparations were being made for a wonderful Christmas Eve, but the question remained whether everyone would get there before the storm. Maria, their oldest granddaughter, was assigned to grinding nuts.

"Grandpa," spoke Maria, "will you fix this nut grinder? It's loose and keeps slipping off the table. There are more walnuts to grind. Every time I crank the handle, it starts to move. I'm afraid it will fall."

"Sure will," Grandpa said optimistically.

Grandpa's mother had brought the old grinder from Italy. It was one of her favorite items she'd packed on the boat. The grinder was used to make the traditional Italian nut rolls for holidays and weddings. If Grandpa couldn't fix it, it probably couldn't be fixed.

"Try it now, Maria. I've tinkered with it a little," said Grandpa. He was surprised it was still loose and didn't fit tightly on the table.

His oldest daughter, standing nearby, said, "I guess it's time to grind them in a modern food chopper. I'll go over to my house and bring it back."

"Not just yet," Grandpa replied, determined to make it work. "Let me try something else."

He took it to his tool shed behind the house that overlooked Wills Creek. It had been flooded in the past, rusting the tools. Grandpa was in need of a few new tools, but the old-timer didn't like to spend money on modern conveniences.

Inside the house, Maria answered the telephone. "It's Uncle Romeo," she told Grandma. Romeo was Grandpa's youngest son. "He's at the mall and would like a gift suggestion for Grandpa. Any ideas?"

Catrina, Romeo's sister, heard the conversation. "What about a nut chopper, blender, or food processor? Something modern to chop nuts with," she suggested.

"Yes, we could use one, but I don't think Grandpa would agree," Grandma said. "He likes the old way of doing things."

Grandpa worked on the nut grinder all day. The early nut rolls were baked, but the remainder were placed aside while other foods were prepared.

The wind picked up and it began to snow on Christmas Eve morning. Apparently, the blizzard predictions were accurate. Family was starting to arrive from several states.

The food preparations were almost finished, except the nut rolls, while Grandpa wouldn't let Catrina bring in her modern nut chopper. He insisted that he'd have the old one fixed soon.

The family would have to spend Christmas Eve without enough traditional nut rolls for everyone. The power went off and by the time it was restored it was too late to make them. All the other great-smelling foods were on the table. The few nut rolls were obviously not enough to feed the large family. After dinner when Grandpa opened his Christmas gift from Romeo, he found a state-of-the-art electric nut chopper.

"Thank you, son. This is something we really need. I'm sorry that we are short of nut rolls tonight. I thought I could fix the old nut grinder, but it's seen its better days. I'll keep it in the shed and cherish it as an antique. I realize now, there's a time and place for modern conveniences. Next holiday, we'll use the new nut chopper."

Grandma managed to slice small slivers of the nut rolls for the family to taste. "Tea or coffee, anyone?" she said with a smile.

GARY'S HOLIDAY DÉJÀ VU

When Oliver Mills updated his insurance coverage, Gary Linford volunteered to take the papers to the Mills' home for signing. Gary had been an agent at Compton Insurance Company for ten years and was eager to see the mansion that was the pride of Cambridge, Ohio.

As Gary parked his car in the circular drive, he marveled at the Greek columns standing at the entrance of the three-story structure. Japanese maple trees and tea roses dotted the flawless lawn. "Such splendor," he muttered, ringing the doorbell.

A portly maid answered the door. "Mr. Mills is expecting you," she said. "Please make yourself comfortable." She pointed to a room on the left.

As Gary entered the room, an eerie sensation overcame him. *I recognize this room*, he thought. *How could that be? The furniture is different, but I've seen this room before.*

A pale blue velvet sofa was against the wall with a matching chair on the other side of the fireplace. The mantel was Italian marble. An elaborate entertainment system occupied the entire opposite wall.

Gary was now looking at a black leather sofa with two matching chairs. The east wall sported a plasma TV and a panoramic painting of Wills Creek in autumn. Norman Rockwell prints covered the west wall.

"I know this is the same room," Gary whispered. "Have I been here before, or was it a dream?"

He crept into the hallway. To his right were two massive hand-carved oak doors with brass handles. Gary knew that a large room, a *grand* room, was behind those doors. He gently pushed one door and peeked inside.

The room easily accommodated the fifty or so people there. Beautiful women in sequined gowns danced to holiday music as men in formal wear sipped champagne and talked about the stock market and sports. The champagne tasted heavenly—Gary had never before drunk anything like it. A Christmas tree, topped with a white satin-robed angel, stood majestically in front of the main window. So many lights! Red and green tinsel dangled from the huge crystal chandelier. Pine wreaths with multi-colored lights graced the windows. Laughter filled the air. Who was laughing so loudly? Was that his own voice?

The room was just as large as he remembered, but there was no Christmas tree, no party, and no champagne. It was now a library of sorts, with three barrister bookcases, two computers, and two desks, one a mammoth rolltop. The piano! Gary quickly looked to his left. There it was, the same baby grand that he had seen before.

Jingle bell, jingle bell, jingle bell rock. Everyone was singing. At least he thought so. He knew that he was singing. Did he really hear someone tell him to get off the piano?

"This is freaking me out," Gary said to himself. "I don't understand any of this."

He strained for an explanation. When he first joined Compton Insurance, Tom Saylor had taught him the ropes. Tom also had taught him how to party with the best of them. Gary spent many mornings kneeling before the porcelain god with little memory of the night before. Thank goodness those days were long gone.

He closed the oak door and stood silently in the hall. He noticed the ornate staircase. Upstairs was a genuine Picasso, he remembered. And the bathroom...

He was chatting with a cute blonde and sipping champagne. Was that his third glass, or fourth? Oh, no! He had to find a bathroom quickly.

"Hello, Gary," greeted Mr. Mills as he descended the staircase.

"Good morning, sir. I have all the paperwork ready and waiting. But first, Mr. Mills, something is bothering me. I don't know if it's déjà vu or if I'm losing my mind. Forgive me for asking, but do you have a brass toilet?"

Oliver Mills stopped in his tracks. His eyes widened and his nostrils flared. He clenched the railing until his knuckles were white. His breathing became fast and heavy. Gary feared he was having a heart attack. Oliver Mills straightened to his full six-feet, three inches and roared at Gary: "So YOU'RE the idiot who ruined my tuba!"

DONNA WELLS

CHRISTMAS WITH THE ADAMS FAMILY

Eugene Adams came into the house, "Well Doris, I finished decorating the trees out front with the multi-colored lights, just like you wanted. How is the menu coming along?"

"I'm just finishing the last batch of cookies and the turkey is cleaned and patiently waiting in the fridge."

"The house looks great. Is there anything I can help you with?"

"You can stop eating my cookies or I'll have to make more before I start to put the stockings together. Would you please run upstairs and grab the stockings?"

"I'm on it. How many do you need?"

"Well, let's see. Six for Jan and her family. Two for Dorothy and Mike. One for Laura and two more for Bobby and his girlfriend. Can't wait to meet her. By the way he talks about her, I wouldn't be a bit surprised to witness a proposal on Christmas day. That means that I'll need eleven stockings."

"I can't wait to see them all. We haven't had all four kids together here in Cambridge for Christmas since they were little. Now that they live out West, we're lucky to see more than one of them at Christmastime. The nearest is near Chicago. You sure you have enough trinkets to fill eleven stockings?"

"Well, I've had this planned for months. Besides their main gifts, I've bought and individually wrapped over 100 items as stocking stuffers. It's just generic small stuff—toothbrushes; small bottles of cologne or shaving cream, depending on gender; post notes; markers; stamps; etc."

"Even the grandkids?"

"Eugene, for crying out loud, they're teenagers. They're not babies anymore. My hands are covered in flour; can you grab the phone?"

Caller ID on the phone shows that the call is from Jan.

"Hi honey, can't wait to see you guys. What? Oh my goodness. Well, you folks just stay put. I've got to hang up now and tell Mother. She is jumping around like a cat on a hot tin roof. Talk to you soon. Love you too."

"Eugene, for crying out loud, what's wrong?"

"Snow."

"What?"

"Snow, and plenty of it. Worst winter storm of the century, according to Jan. Everything from Chicago on west is buried under it. Nothing is moving. No buses, cars, or airplanes, and even the trains are grounded. Roads from Chicago to California are closed. The storm is moving this way. By nightfall tomorrow, Christmas night, it will hit Cambridge."

"Well," said Doris, "there isn't a thing we can do about it. Let's grab a cup of coffee and watch the weather report."

"Won't be the same without any kids at all. I was really looking forward to the holiday. Wait a minute," said Eugene. "I have an idea."

"Me too," said Doris. "What is your idea?"

"No, Doris, you did most of the work. You go first."

"Well, tomorrow you know the phone will be ringing off the wall, what with the kids checking on us to make sure we're okay. So what if we call them first and wish them each a Merry Christmas, 'cause tomorrow we are going to be all over Cambridge delivering good cheer to our Meals-on-Wheels shut-ins."

Eugene laughed, "That is exactly what I was thinking. We can pass out the stockings and, if we run out of stockings, we can pass out some of that mountain of cookies you've been working on all week. I'm sure if our family can't get here there are plenty of others whose families cannot travel because of the weather."

Eugene and Doris Adams spent Christmas day buzzing around Cambridge. They finished their stops just as the snow started. They made it home just before dark, feeling tired but happy and, most of all, useful.

JUNE COMES HOME

Mandy Oliver, 45, a blue-eyed, brown-haired woman, is looking out the window of her mother's room in the Wills Creek Valley Hospital. It is Christmas Eve. The falling snow covers the street and sidewalks. The Christmas decorations hanging on nearby homes blow in a strong north wind. The Nativity on the lawn of the Wills Creek Care Center, across the street, is swiftly being covered by the falling snow.

The snow reminds Mandy of the Christmases of her childhood. She remembers visiting relatives, school and church Christmas programs. She especially remembers Christmases at Grandma and Grandpa Miller's. She and her cousins, Jane and Paul, enjoyed drinking hot chocolate in her Aunt Susan's kitchen after an afternoon outside sled riding, ice skating, or building snowmen.

Mandy's mother, June Snyder, is recuperating from breast cancer surgery. In addition, she has pneumonia, which sometimes occurs as a complication of surgery. She sits up in bed. She is wearing a pink robe, which compliments her white hair. "Mandy, what do you see?"

"I see falling snow, covering everything, even the street. People are entering our church for the Christmas Eve service too. The Christmas lights are reflecting on the creek. It's so beautiful."

Mrs. Snyder sighs, "I wish we were able to go to the service tonight. The choir's voices remind me of Heaven and angels singing." Suddenly, Mrs. Snyder gasps for air. Mandy pushes the red call button to summon help. The Respiratory Response Team rushes to the room to put an oxygen mask on her. In spite of their efforts to help her, she lapses into unconsciousness, breathing very shallowly.

Tears streaming down her face, Mandy follows Dr. Glenn to the Intensive Care Unit counseling room. He begins by saying, "Mandy, your mother's lungs are filling with fluid. We can give her medicine to help ease the pain, but her lungs and heart are shutting down. She probably won't live until morning."

Mandy cries quietly, holding Dr. Glenn's hand for comfort. They hold hands as he prays for her mother. Later, he leaves, driving through the falling snow.

Rev. Grimm takes a seat beside Mandy to console her. "Mandy, your mother is a Christian. You know without doubt that she will immediately be with Jesus in Heaven."

"I know that's true, but still it's hard to let her go. I'll miss her so much. I don't want to see her suffer anymore. The breast cancer is causing a lot of pain. She knew that chemotherapy and radiation treatments were to follow her surgery. She was positively thinking she would survive and live to see her family continue to grow."

After Rev. Grimm leaves, Mandy kneels by her mother's bed and prays, asking God for His will to be done. She feels a strange warming sensation spread through her from the top of her head to the tips of her toes. Her mother awakens and tries to talk. Mandy stands up and removes the oxygen mask.

Her mother cries out, "Where am I? What's going on?"

Mandy looks at her in astonishment. "Mom, you're in the hospital. You had cancer surgery. You were unconscious and near death."

"Mandy, I'm hungry. I want to go home!"

"Mom," replies Mandy, "we have to make sure you're well enough to go home."

There is a knock on the door. Dr. Glenn enters. He glances at the two women talking. "What's happened? June, you look amazing!"

"That's why I want to go home for Christmas. I dreamed that Jesus said, 'June, go home. Your mansion isn't ready. Finish your work.' I woke up and now I'm ready to go home."

Dr. Glenn examines June. Her vital signs are normal and her lungs are clear. "If you promise to obey my instructions, you can go home tonight," he promises.

"Thank you, doctor. I can't wait to tell them I saw Jesus and he sent me home. Someday I'll go to my heavenly home, but not tonight."

Mandy is standing transfixed, shedding tears of joy. Mom is going home!

CAREY MOZENA

MAMA'S RIBBONS

Mama was strange. I know every family has their own Christmas traditions. My best friend had to wait until after pictures were taken before opening any gifts. The kids next door were allowed to open one gift Christmas Eve. Not us, though. My three sisters and I had to save the ribbon on top of our Christmas gift. Since there were so many of us and Mama never had much money, we kids only got one gift each Christmas. Our one gift was always a new doll that Mama made herself.

The dolls were nice, but saving the ribbon on the gift was just plain dumb. Mama never reused the ribbons; she made new ones every year. She also made new name tags. Mama drew the tags, complete with the year on each one, and then tied the tags to the ribbons and saved each one every year.

That was just one of Mama's strange quirks. For some reason, that tradition stuck in my head ever since the funeral. We buried Mama less than a month before Christmas. I didn't think it would be the same without Mama this year. Mama always brought the family together.

My sisters and I are all grown and married. Two of them even have grandchildren. Last week, we all got together at the old farmhouse in Wills Creek, trying to figure out what to do with all of Mama's old things. Being the youngest, I was voted to go through the attic.

There were boxes everywhere! I never knew that Mama had collected so much junk. Wiping the dust off one, I unfolded the flaps and peered inside. It was filled with scraps of paper that had yellowed with age. I rolled my eyes and turned to another dusty box. This one was filled with old lace and faded wood. I coughed as I tried to pull a handful out and stirred up more dust. Why did Mama keep all this garbage?

Frustrated, I pulled another faded box into the dim light and opened it. I stared at what was inside. Reaching in, I carefully pulled out the crushed curls of an old ribbon that had been on a Christmas gift. Squinting at the tag, I read: *"To: Mary Ann, with love, 1977."* It was the ribbon that had been on my gift the year I turned ten years old. The memory of that Christmas came back to me. I remembered all the fun we had caroling for the neighbors with our new dolls. I dug into the box and pulled out more ribbons, each one faded, but readable. This one was a keeper.

I went back to the box that had the faded wood in it and, holding my breath, I pulled out a piece that was wrapped in lace and uncovered it. It was an ink drawing in a wooden frame that Mama had done over fifty years ago! The lace kept it from fading too badly. I pulled out more framed drawings that Mama had done. Several had stains or were faded from age, but each one brought back another memory of Mama. Rewrapping and repacking the drawings, I turned back to the first box that held the paper scraps.

I took the top scrap and held it up to the light, recognizing Mama's handwriting right away. The writing on it described a Christmas past, and another scrap told of her wedding day. There were cuttings from old newspapers too, and I realized that these scraps were Mama's version of a diary.

I took the boxes home with me and set up Mama's ink drawings all over the living room, arranged the diary papers in a photo album along with some of my own photos, and decorated the Christmas tree with the old ribbons. I invited my sisters and their families over for Christmas this year. It was amazing. It was like Mama was right there with us again.

EVELYN HILEMAN

AN UNPLANNED DAY OF VOLUNTEERING

Kelly looked around her house, seeing many things that needed her attention. The checkbook on the desk said, "Balance me." The potted palm tree by the register said, "Water me." The dishwasher said, "Empty me." Her nails said, "Trim me." The Christmas cards said, "Send me," and the boxes of tree trimmings in the corner said, "Time to decorate." How would she ever get everything done on this one-day-off-in two weeks?

Kelly was glad for the overtime at The Wills Creek Medical Clinic but, with the holidays, she needed more hours in her day. Up early, planning to cross the "must do's" off her list as fast as she could, she put away the dishes then cleaned her glasses to work on the checkbook. The phone rang. She let the answering machine play and heard, "This is Ann Pierce at the Salvation Army and we need more workers at the Food Pantry. Two of our usual helpers have colds and shouldn't be near food. If you can help, please call me! Everyone says they're so busy that sometimes it seems we've forgotten what Christmas celebrates." She ended with a telephone number.

If only she hadn't added "Everyone says they're so busy that sometimes it seems we've forgotten what Christmas celebrates..." Kelly balanced the checkbook. *I could probably give an hour to the Food Pantry and still get most of my list completed, she thought.* She called Ann to say she was leaving right away.

Her job at the Food Pantry was not a difficult one, putting paper liners on each tray and stacking them. The room smelled good as the food heated and a line of people filed past. The "joy of giving" spirit was certainly in that room and showed on the faces of the food handlers.

As soon as she saw the end of the line, Kelly put on her coat. "Thanks for helping us out with short notice," Ann thanked her.

"You're welcome. I see that a lot goes into what was done here today," Kelly responded.

As she walked down the hall toward the parking lot, Kelly saw a gathering of people through an open door. Then she noticed the boxes lined up on many tables in a large room. As she passed by, a cheerful voice called out, "Oh good! Another helper. Come right on in."

"No, I helped in the Food Pantry and I have to leave now," Kelly explained.

"Many hands make light work, the Amish say, and we have many holiday boxes to fill if you could help... We have to fill and deliver all these boxes today. It's Christmastime, you know," the volunteer leader said.

With the deadline of this friendly group, her chores seemed less important. "Oh, all right, but I didn't plan on being here today."

How organized they are, Kelly observed. One volunteer set out foodstuff items, another person maintained a list. After an item was placed in each box, that item was crossed off the list. Everyone was busy, yet they seemed to enjoy their task.

"Put these gloves on. The hams are cold and you'll need them," the leader explained. Kelly was the "ham girl." Next she became the "potato girl," placing a bag of potatoes on the bottom of each box. Then she was "cereal girl." Time went fast and several hours later she told the group she had to head for home. "We'll miss you. Thanks for your help," a lady said.

"Would it help if I delivered a box or two on my way home?" Kelly couldn't believe she said it. She had truly forgotten about her personal Christmas list and had found true enjoyment in her unplanned day of volunteering.

The families were home when she made two deliveries. Their smiles of appreciation said *"Thanks."*

At home, she watered the palm tree and crossed that off her long list. But her heart was lighter. She learned that day what Christmas actually means.

LINDA WARRICK

SMALL TOWN BLESSINGS

The blizzard gripping the Ohio Valley had let up, but the roads were still treacherous. Jason knew that he must get to work.

He, his wife, and two little ones rented a farmhouse in the country along the banks of Wills Creek. It was a beautiful setting anytime of the year, but hard to get into and out of during inclement weather. With too much rain, the valleys were prone to flooding. Too much snow, and it was nearly impassable, especially if it drifted. Freezing rain was downright dangerous, given the narrow country roads, steep hills, and few guardrails. How he wished he'd been able to afford something closer to town, but it wasn't an option now. Melanie did not work outside the home, since they only had one vehicle and the children to care for.

The family depended on Jason. They needed the overtime on his next paycheck to get through the holidays. The children were six and four and excited to see what Santa would bring. He just couldn't let them down. They hadn't been able to do any shopping yet; there was just never anything left. Jason's parents were gone now and Melanie's father was in a rest home. Her mother had abandoned her when she was ten.

It seemed they were alone in the world. But Jason was a hard worker. He had been working two jobs to get by, that is until the plant closed.

The old Chevy fishtailed up the first small hill. As he rounded the curve at the bottom of the down side of the hill, the car skidded off the road and rolled down an embankment. It came to rest upside down in a snowbank alongside the creek. The impact knocked Jason unconscious. All of a sudden, he felt his spirit rise from his body and, from just above the accident, he watched the scene as if he were a spectator. He noticed the snow falling again, wondering how he was going to upright the car and get out of there. A deer peered from behind the grove of trees. Oh, she had a little one with her. After what was actually hours, the doe slowly approached the wreckage, perhaps as much out of curiosity as looking for food.

Taking a closer look, Jason saw that the driver's side door had come open and his body lay partially in the snow. Time seemed to stand still. *Would help ever come?* As he watched, the doe crept over to him and, miraculously, began licking his face. He felt as if he were being jerked back into his body as he came into consciousness. The doe jumped back with a start and ran into the woods.

Reeling from the trauma and his head pounding, Jason moved steadily to wiggle free of his confines. He thought his leg must be broken. Raising himself up and through the broken window, he crawled up the embankment, dragging the injured leg behind him. If he stayed below and waited, no one may ever find him.

He lay alongside the road waiting, praying aloud that nothing more serious was wrong, given the pain he was in. After what seemed like hours, he heard the rumble of a car coming in his direction.

At the hospital, his leg was set. He was kept overnight for observation, then released a few days before Christmas.

A reporter from the Wills Creek Tribune interviewed Jason's wife about the accident and published the story on the front page. Soon, friends and even strangers gathered at the family's home with gifts of food, toys, and money. Pleasant Valley Motors donated a used four-wheel drive vehicle to replace the demolished Chevy. The community wanted to make sure Jason and his family had a wonderful holiday.

"I guess there really is a Santa, and he lives right here in Guernsey County," said Jason with a grateful heart. "I've even seen his reindeer!"

PAM RITCHEY

A BREAK FROM BASIC

The drill sergeant wasn't happy to see Mandy Thompson that day in late November. The United States Army frowns upon spouses relocating until their mates complete basic training and receive their duty orders. Never one to be apart from her husband, especially at Christmas, Mandy left their home along Wills Creek and followed when Dave enlisted.

Even though the rules stated no visitors were allowed during basic training, she thought of a scheme to work around them. By setting up a checking account in only her husband's name, she was frequently able to spend brief bits of time with him while he signed checks for their bills.

Soon the other recruits came to dread the sight of Mandy's car pulling into the parking lot. A quick dash would be made to hide any contraband snacks because their drill sergeant, Sgt. Moore, would do a spot inspection and confiscate any cookies or candy to give to her and Dave's five-year-old twins, Makala and Zipporah. He loved spoiling them.

Mandy soon found a small furnished apartment near the base entrance. The only things she took on the long journey to Ft. Sill, Oklahoma, were necessities that would fit in the smallest U-Haul trailer they made. Most of their belongings either were sold or in storage back in Ohio.

With Christmas approaching, Mandy wracked her brain to come up with presents for her twins and husband. Relocation funds were long gone, and a new private's paycheck only went so far. Even a Christmas tree seemed out of reach.

Looking through a sales circular from a local shopping center, Mandy spied a Raggedy Ann doll on sale. *I can make that*, she thought to herself.

Digging through their meager belongings, she located a pillowcase, unraveled a crocheted potholder, and popped some buttons off an old blouse. In a few days, she had created her own version of the dolls, complete with yarn hair and button eyes. A magic marker took care of rosy cheeks and red lips. The blouse transformed into cute little dresses.

While checking out help wanted ads in the newspaper, her eyes wandered to the pet listings. A fellow Army family was giving away their golden retriever because of a transfer. Dave always talked about wanting one, so with a quick call, his gift was taken care of.

But what about a tree? We have to have a Christmas tree!
A trip to the commissary on base solved that problem. There beside the baking needs was a small two-foot tree, ornaments and lights included, for only $5. Mandy and the twins ate a few extra peanut butter and jelly sandwiches to make up for the cost.

Now all that was needed for a wonderful Christmas was the man of the house. Hopefully, the rumored Christmas leave would materialize.

The night before Christmas Eve, Mandy put the twins to bed with a sad heart. Dave's last phone call had dashed any hope of him being home for Christmas. Sgt. Moore informed them there would be no leave and no visitations for Christmas. This would be the first Christmas they spent apart.

"Mommy, does Daddy get to come home for Christmas?" Makala asked as her mother tucked her in.

"No, Sweetheart, not this year," she replied, trying to put on a brave front. "It's okay though; we'll see him in a few days and take Christmas to him!"

Mandy went to bed early and said a prayer for God to change the Army's mind. Tossing and turning, she had trouble sleeping. While rearranging her pillows, a loud knock on the door echoed through the small apartment.

Who could it be? It's 1:00 a.m.!
Pulling the curtain aside, she was thrilled to see her husband standing on the porch with a duffle bag slung over his shoulder.

"How did you...? What are you...? You're not..." Mandy couldn't finish a sentence as Dave took her in his arms, twirling her around the room.

"Sgt. Moore came in at midnight, woke us up, and gave us our leave papers! I'm yours until January 2nd," he said between kisses.

The Thompson's had a very happy Christmas in their new home.

BEVERLY WENCEK KERR

GLOWING GIFT

One package under Jimmy's Christmas tree actually glowed! A long red box gleamed as he peeked under the branches of twinkling lights before everyone else got up. *What could it be? A lamp that turned on by accident? Maybe those neat twisted lights shifted when the package moved?* To add to the mystery, he couldn't find a name tag. *Where did it come from?*

Jimmy could hardly wait for his mom and dad to wake up so the gift could be opened. Of course, he hoped it was for him, but he never ever saw a present glowing.

He drifted off to sleep beside the tree, dreaming of fun presents his parents couldn't afford. Dad lost his job at Wills Creek Packaging a few weeks earlier, making money for Christmas scarce. That meant fewer gifts this year.

In his dream, Jimmy rode a new bicycle down Claysville Road. Then he saw a skateboard by the side of the road and hopped on it. Next, he raced on horseback through the pasture field and over a fence. He loved to go fast and enjoyed doing tricks. He was riding the horse and jumping over a tall tree when he awoke with a start.

Mom and Dad were finally awake! Now he could see inside that mysterious package shining like a jar of lightning bugs.

When they entered the room, they acted as surprised as Jimmy. Mom said, "Where did that gleaming package come from? I have never seen a present all lit up like that before."

Dad scratched his head, saying, "Beats me!" They exchanged looks and shrugged their shoulders.

There weren't many packages under the tree this year, but they always saved the best until last. By the time they unwrapped all the presents except the shining one, Jimmy could contain himself no longer. When he reached for the package, he saw a name tag that said JIMMY.

Anxiously, he tore the red paper off the glowing box. A sparkling blue skateboard! Just what he wanted. "Can I go outside and try it out?" he shouted.

Slipping into his tennis shoes, Jimmy hurried out the door, still wearing his warm sweats. With the new board under his arm, he went flying down to the sidewalk. He never had a skateboard of his own before, but he had used his friend Eric's. First he tried just cruising down the walk. The skateboard still glowed.

Next he attempted some tricks. He could do them without even trying. The skateboard seemed to do them all by itself, like magic. *Hmmm, perhaps that's why it glowed! Maybe the skateboard was magic.*

"This is totally awesome," exclaimed Jimmy.

From then on, he did every trick imaginable, while his mom and dad watched in amazement from inside the front door. Jimmy did a Backside Shuvit, a Frontside 180, and even a Kickflip. Whatever Jimmy tried doing, the skateboard did.

"Hey, Dad!" called Jimmy. "Could we go to the Cambridge Skate Park and try this board out on the ramps?"

"Sounds like fun," said Dad. "Get your coats and let's go." The three of them piled in the old pickup and headed across town to the skate park.

Now Jimmy went up and down the sloping curves with ease and even rode the rail. He could do The Ollie up curbs and steps. His smiling face said he felt on top of the world.

When they returned home, Jimmy jumped out of the pickup truck begging, "Please let me go to Eric's so I can show him my new skateboard!"

Dad replied, "Sure son, have fun." Jimmy grabbed his board and headed to his friend's house.

When Dad and Mom sat down at the kitchen table, Mom said, "That is no ordinary skateboard and this was no ordinary Christmas. It's puzzling."

Nodding his head, Dad agreed while dipping a sugar cookie in his coffee. "Did you buy that skateboard?" he asked.

"Well, no," said Mom. "I thought maybe you did. Where did it come from and how did it get under the tree?"

Sometimes you just have to believe in magic.

A Good Deed Returned
A Hundred fold

Walking up to the door of St. Stephen Catholic Church, Donald stopped before entering. Opening the doors, he paused to let his eyes adjust to the dim lights and flickering candles. The church was almost empty, except for some old ladies praying the rosary in the front pews. The church was decorated for Christmas with pine roping and red bows. The heavy aroma of incense permeated his nose as he sat down in the last pew.

Precisely at 7:00 p.m., the light over the confessional came on. Three ladies in the front pew lined up to enter.

I wonder what sins they have, he thought. *They can hardly walk.* After a few minutes the line was empty. *It's now or never*, he thought as he walked down the aisle.

Kneeling down, Donald crossed himself. "Forgive me, Father, for I have sinned."

"How long has it been since your last confession, my son?"

"I can't remember, Father. Years, it's been many years."

"Go on."

"Father, I repaid good with evil. I stole from people who only wanted to help me." Sobbing, Donald paused to regain his composure. "I don't know where to begin. I'm so ashamed."

"Maybe this isn't the place to discuss this, my son. Would it be possible for you to come to the Rectory after Mass? We will have more time to talk."

"That might be better," Donald replied.

Later that evening, Donald walked across the lawn to the church rectory. Ringing the door bell, he was surprised to see the man who answered. He wasn't anything like he expected; before him stood an old redheaded man in a jogging suit.

"Hi, I'm Father Robert. I presume you are the person I talked to earlier tonight?"

"Yes, Father. I'm Donald McBeth. Thanks for seeing me."

"Let's talk in my study," Father Robert suggested. "Maybe a glass of sherry would help you relax. I find it helps me after trying days, and we have had a lot of them lately."

Pouring two glasses of wine, Father Robert reached for his vestment, draping them around his shoulders. "Remember, my son, anything you tell me here is as if you told me in the confessional."

"I don't know where to start," Donald said.

"Why not from the beginning, Donald? Leave nothing out. Confession is good for the soul."

"My parents owned an M&K Grocery Store on the banks of Wills Creek in Pleasant City. I delivered groceries after school. Most of my deliveries were to older people and widow women. They always had money lying around. I started just taking a nickel or dime, but it escalated to larger amounts. This went on for years. I was never caught. To make matters worse, at Christmas they always gave me cookies and candy. This has been eating at me for years. I've done well in life: the Mercedes in the parking is mine. How can I make up for what I did? Those people are all gone now. I can't forgive myself, Father."

"God will forgive you, my son, but first you must forgive yourself. Go and pray in the church. You will find your answer there."

The next week passed quickly for Father Robert as he made preparations for Midnight Mass. For many, it wouldn't be a happy Christmas since the Glass Plant closed. Stopping at the Wills Creek Times to pick up his newspaper, he was astounded by the hustle and bustle around town.

'What's all the excitement?" he asked the editor. "I haven't seen this much activity in town in years."

"Haven't you heard?" the editor replied. "Someone went around town last night slipping $100 bills under people's doors. So far, over forty people have found them."

"It's a miracle. It's a miracle," Father Robert said.

Later that evening, Father Robert smiled as he opened a card and a new hundred dollar bill fell out.

The message was short. 'God answers prayer.' Signed, *Donald.*

KIZZY'S QUESTION

Christmas in the middle of summer? It's 92 degrees and muggy as a basset hound's muzzle. Kizzy Carmichael pulled the damp auburn curls up off her neck into a banana clip. It left her looking like a rooster; her red hair sticking straight up, a chinless face, and that beak she'd hated since childhood.

It's too darn hot, she pouted. *There're good reasons it's celebrated in December.* She wished Deirdre hadn't talked her into helping organize Wills Creek Church's "Christmas in July" fundraiser.

"There you are, Kizzy." Aggie Masterson, a large woman who always wore a warm smile, had no sense of decorum. She flumped into the pew beside Kizzy, rocking it backward, giving Kizzy a momentary bout of vertigo. "You working on the fundraiser?"

"Yeah, meeting's tonight. I'm sitting here where it's cool, trying to think. Got any ideas, Aggie?"

"Make sure there's chocolate, m'dear—the most important part of Christmas. If there's chocolate, every woman in the church will be here, and that makes a good fundraiser."

"Thanks, I hadn't thought of that." Kizzy pulled a spiral notebook and pen from her pocket. "Chocolate—first thing on the list."

"Glad to help." Aggie struggled to her feet, waddling toward the pastor's office. *No doubt she's got some advice for him too*—Kizzy couldn't help the irreverent thought.

Straight-laced old Audrey McElroy poked her head around the doorway, looking down through spinster glasses over a very straight sharp nose. "You still here, girl?"

"Just brainstorming ideas for the fundraiser, Mrs. McElroy. What do they usually do at these things?"

"My heavens, they raise funds, of course."

"Of course. But I mean, what about activities?"

"Well, the choir sings. Without Christmas music it wouldn't seem like

Christmas, now would it?" Mrs. McElroy disappeared down the hall.

'Caroling by choir,' Kizzy noted. *The choir director can handle that.*

Stretching, she absentmindedly picked lint from the pew cushion. *Oh, we'll need a clean-up crew.* She scribbled a note and poked the notebook in her pocket. Wandering into the foyer, she found Caroline Finley, a young mother-to-be, juggling a large box, her purse, and car keys.

"I'll help, Carrie," offered Kizzy. Relieving Carrie of the cumbersome carton, she asked, "Where to?"

"Library. Uncle Charles cleared out his spare room and donated books. What're you doing here today, Kizzy?"

"Meditating, where it's cool, before the fundraiser meeting. Something I can't put my finger on is bugging me. I guess it's just hard to think Christmas in hot weather."

"Yeah," Caroline puffed, plopping into a plush maroon armchair. "I love the food though! What're they having this year?"

"Don't know yet. I'll bring it up." Kizzy made a mental note. "Anything else?"

"Crafts! Let's make new ornaments for the tree." Kizzy retrieved her notebook and wrote 'food' and 'ornaments.'

"I haven't been to the meeting yet but my list is sure growing," she laughed. Carrie rose from her seat, jingling her keys. Kizzy's eyes popped like toadstools. "Omigosh!—Almost forgot Santa!"

"And elves," added Carrie. "Well, I'm off—home to put my feet up."

"You really look tired, Carrie. I'll come by to help you tomorrow, okay? Hmm, that reminds me, what about a service activity?" Her pencil flew over the paper.

Waving goodbye at the door, Kizzy whirled around, almost crashing into Deirdre McIntire, the pillar of the women's group, as she whizzed past. "Meeting in fifteen, Kizzy!"

Kizzy leaned against the bulletin board, reviewing her notes. "Chocolate, caroling, setup, food, ornaments, Santa, elves, service… something's missing. What is it?"

Pastor Carmichael, Bible in hand, smiled and bobbed his head courteously as he passed.

"Christmas! That's it!" Kizzy squealed, causing the good pastor to jump a foot in the air. "Sorry, Pastor. I just remembered…we have to invite the guest of honor!" In large letters across the top of her paper, she wrote 'C-H-R-I-S-T.' *That's what we need in Christmas!*

JERRY WOLFROM

SANTA WORE PLAID SHORTS

There was no mistaking the time of year. Salvation Army volunteers were vigorously ringing bells in front of the Wills Valley Supermart. Shoppers were emerging through the double doors, pushing carts heaped with Christmas food.

Time was short; Christmas was two days away. Inside, employees wore Santa hats. Carts were gridlocked in most aisles. Holiday sweets and snacks were prominently displayed and Christmas music was in the air.

She appeared to be about 30 and fit the description of the perfect soccer mom. Her clean jeans and top matched; her long blonde hair in a neat ponytail. The little girl with her was about eight, the boy about seven. Both were dressed in worn but freshly-laundered clothes.

As the trio made their way down the first aisle, it was apparent the soccer mom was buying food for their Christmas dinner. She carefully examined the price tag on every package before either dropping it into her cart or placing it back on the shelf. The kids asked for several items, but she usually shook her head with, "Can't afford it right now."

The three inched toward the rear, pausing to look at dinner rolls. As they checked prices, they were approached by an unkempt little man wearing a thin t-shirt and outrageous green checkered shorts, not the most appropriate attire for a bitterly cold December day in Ohio. He hadn't shaved in weeks and his unbrushed salt-and-pepper hair fell to his shoulders. There were large holes in his dirty sneakers.

In a friendly tone he asked, "Finding any bargains?"

"Trying to," she grinned. "I have to count my pennies."

The man nodded then continued toward the meat section. A few minutes later, he looked up to find the soccer mom and the kids carefully searching the frozen food bin for a turkey.

Smiling, she said to him, "I need a really large turkey. I have three more kids at home to feed."

"And don't forget Daddy," the little boy reminded her.

She managed a weak smile. "My husband's a coal miner. He got laid off down at the Cumberland strip mines and he had to take a job over in Powhatan. Really long drive. Then, two months ago, they closed that mine, too."

"Ouch!" the man grimaced.

Later, the mother pushed her cart, both baskets piled high, into the checkout line. There were no boxes of the more expensive foods. Mostly, she had selected fresh fruits and vegetables, along with all of the regular staples.

The old guy glanced at her heaping cart. *Guess I forgot how much food it takes to feed a family of six*, he mused.

It took the cashier several minutes to ring up the contents in the soccer mom's cart. She handed him a blue-green card, which was placed on the register.

"A hundred twenty-six dollars," the clerk said, swiping the card. Then, pausing, he swiped it again. "Uh, oh," he said, "There's only eleven dollars left on your card."

"But, there has to be a mistake," the soccer mom whispered.

"Sorry, no. Do you have cash or a check?"

"No. I'll have to go home to see if my husband has any money. What about this food?"

"We'll hold it in the back room until closing time."

Shocked and embarrassed, the soccer mom hustled her little ones toward the parking lot, tears rolling down her cheeks. She refused to explain the situation to the curious children. They wouldn't understand. As she reached her car, a fifteen-year-old clunker with rusty fenders and no hubcaps, a voice behind her called out, "Just a minute, ma'am." Turning, she saw the old guy in green shorts pushing her loaded cart toward her. "Back seat or trunk?"

"But...."

"No buts, young lady. Dry your tears and get home to the rest of your family. And have a very merry Christmas."

"I'll pay you back," she stammered. "What's your name?"

"Claus, ma'am. Santa Claus," he grinned crookedly. "Next time you're at the North Pole, stop in and see me."

Then he was gone.

HARRIETTE ORR

THE PERFECT TREE

Here it is three weeks before Christmas and we're off to buy our live Christmas tree. One by one, we pile into the old Dodge station wagon: my older brother Ricky, sister Ellie, and me, Cindy. Duchess, our black Lab, claims her spot in the back and Mom is at the wheel. The weather is bright and crisp, a perfect day.

We head out of Cambridge over the viaduct, a cement humpback bridge which carries you up over the railroad tracks and Wills Creek. Soon we are pulling in to the tree farm high on a hill north of Fairdale. As we exit the wagon, we are hit in the face by a sharp wind peppered with a hint of sleet.

"Oh no," exclaims Mom. "It is going to rain! Hurry! Come on, we'll find a tree before it gets too bad."

Off we go, with Ellie and Duchess in the lead. We look at tree after tree and nothing seems just right. They are too big or too small, crooked, or too bare. After trudging around the hill for about a half hour, Mom is grouchy and we are getting weary, not to say a little wet. We finally decide on a tree. Ricky goes to get the man to cut it down for us. In the meantime, the rain is coming down with a vengeance. Mom hurries to pay for the tree while we kids carry it down the hill. Duchess jumps into the back as we pull down the tailgate. But as we start to put the tree inside, Duchess decides to leap out and knocks the tree to the ground. It is raining harder now and we hurry to stuff the tree and the dog back into the wagon.

The tree is left on our front porch where, on the next Friday evening, Ricky and Mom try to fit it into what he calls, "the tree stand from Hell." It has three legs. Each leg has a sharp hook which is pounded into the tree trunk. It is not an easy job to get it to stand straight. After sawing off the bottom, they finally get it upright and there it is—the most perfect tree.

But wait! It's leaning to one side. Down it goes again. Ricky struggles to pound the one leg in further. We stand it up again. It looks better, but Mom says, "What is this? Oh, my gosh! The back of the tree got covered with mud when it fell out of the wagon."

Have you ever tried to get frozen mud off a tree? We had to take buckets of warm water and towels and hand rub it free of mud before it could be brought into the house to thaw out and dry.

Saturday, we decided it was ready to decorate. When we got it into the corner of the room, it wanted to lean forward. Mom hammered nails into the window frame and then wound fishing line around the trunk of the tree and back around the nails. Magazines were stacked under one leg to make it level.

On went the strings of lights of many colors. Then the ornaments were lovingly unpacked one by one and placed on the branches. Mom supervised the decorating and was strict about the strands of silver tinsel that were placed just so, three or four at a time over the branches. We kids thought it was much more fun to throw the tinsel and see where it landed. We stood back to admire our work as Mom placed the angel on top. The tree was lit, and there it was, the most beautiful tree ever. To look at it you would think it was perfect. No one would ever know what we went through to bring this about, unless of course, we tell the story time and time again.

DICK METHENEY

IT IS BETTER TO GIVE
THAN TO RECEIVE

The real meaning of Christmas was reinforced during a blizzard in the winter of 1962. My wife, newborn son, and I were living in a three-room apartment above an empty store in Byesville. The gas space heater in the apartment ran non-stop and it barely kept the living room warm. In the bedroom, you could see your breath.

I had been laid off from work for nearly eight months and Christmas was looking bleak, to say the least. By taking every part-time job I could find, I made my six months of unemployment compensation last nine months. With only three more checks coming, we could not afford to spend any money for Christmas.

In the process of moving our bed into the living room to be closer to the heater, I had discovered among our belongings several books of S&H Green Stamps and three books of Top Value Stamps. These stamps were redeemable for merchandise at different area stores and redemption stores in the area.

A week before Christmas, with an unemployment check and our stamp books in hand, we braved the elements and went to do our shopping. It took some time and serious thought to get our meager resources to cover everyone on our shopping list.

There was a fuzzy teddy bear for our son. Each of our mothers got a necklace and matching earring sets. My wife's father got a new set of guitar strings and my father got a screwdriver set because he could never find a screwdriver when he needed one. This got everyone else something but there was nothing left to use to get each other a gift.

That week I undercoated three cars. After purchasing the materials and brushes and spending a whole day on each vehicle, I cleared about $25 each. This was done by hand painting Rustoleum paint on the undercarriage of the vehicle. When the paint had dried, I also applied the undercoat material with a brush. That was not much money for spending eight to ten hours on a mechanic's creeper under a car in the wintertime. But the situation being what it was, I was grateful for the opportunity.

As I drove along Wills Creek on the way home, I saw it was frozen over and covered with snow. I was amazed to see the lights on in the empty store beneath our apartment and people moving tables and cots into the empty space.

"What is going on downstairs? There are people all over the place."

My wife answered, "The landlord came up to tell us he is going to allow a neighborhood church to use the store for a homeless shelter over the holidays. All the existing shelters are full, so they are going to use the kitchen to prepare meals and set up cots for people to sleep on at night."

"How did you get it so warm in here?"

"When they turned the heat on downstairs, it warmed our apartment up."

"This place has not been this warm since October."

That night the temperature dropped to a record low and it started snowing. By 8:00 a.m. on Christmas Eve morning there was 16 inches of snow. At noon, the landlord showed up to plow the parking lot and shovel the sidewalks despite the continued snowing.

At 4:00 p.m., the landlord knocked on our door in a panic. The shelter was supposed to open in an hour and start serving hot meals, but no one from the church could get through the 30 inches of snow. Could we come downstairs and help him with the kitchen until someone could get there to help?

That Christmas evening the three of us, plus our three-month-old son, cooked and served 52 meals to the homeless. After all the customers had fallen asleep, warm and well-fed for the first time in days, the three of us were sitting in the kitchen around a prep table talking about the evening's events. To show his appreciation for our help, the landlord gave us a month's free rent.

That old saying is right, it is better to give than to receive.

DONA McCONNELL

THE GIFT OF BELIEF

I don't want a stuffed cat!" Ava cried. "Molly will be back soon."

The child's parents eyed each other with concern. They'd plotted to pass the toy section of Rubles Department Store, steering toward the stuffed animals. Christmas was only two weeks away and they were panicking. *What do you give a child who wants something no amount of money can buy?*

Ever since Molly died suddenly of feline leukemia, their daughter had been inconsolable. From the time the kitten appeared at their door, skinny and starving, the two were true soul mates. While most cats fear the sudden, staccato movements of children, the kitten leapt with abandon into Ava's arms. The girl was entranced by the cat's calico coat (she called it "rainbow fur") and comical black mustache.

Ava's parents were increasingly concerned at her insistence Molly would be back by Christmas. The child was old enough to understand death but, in Molly's case, the normal rules didn't seem to apply.

"Honey, your cat's gone," her mother said. "She can't come back. Remember when Grammy Lewis went to Heaven? That's where Molly went too."

"She's coming back," Ava declared forcefully, putting a period on the conversation.

"How do you know?" her worried father asked.

"Because she told me. At the vet's. She said she had to go away for a while, but she'd be back."

"Honey, I didn't hear her say anything."

"That's because she said it to *me*, inside my head." The child gave her father a look of exasperation. "It's Christmas, Daddy. Anything can happen at Christmas."

As the air around their home on Wills Creek turned frigid, Ava's parents became more anxious. It didn't help that the child's room was filled with pictures of her and her pet. In almost every one, Molly was licking Ava's eyelid, a funny proclivity that always made the little girl giggle.

The trip to Dr. Bradford was a disaster. No matter how reasoned the doctor's approach, Ava continued her assertion that Molly was returning for Christmas. The doctor used scary words like psychotic break, but Ava seemed like a normal little girl in every other way.

As they wound around City Park Lake, their daughter suddenly squealed. "There she is!"

Ava flung open the door before her father hit the brake. She stumbled, but was quickly upright and headed for the lake.

"Ava!" her parents screamed in unison. "Stop!"

The girl was already at the lake's edge and, to her parents' horror, rushing into the icy water.

"Avaaaa!"

But she was already waist deep, a joyful smile on her face.

Both parents saw it at the same time. A tiny animal, barely hanging onto a floating branch. The water was up to Ava's shoulders as one arm reached toward the twigs. She surged forward in one huge leap. Just then her parents caught up, lifting her out of the water. They wept with relief and pulled her close.

"What were you thinking?" her mother sobbed.

"Stop, Mom," Ava yelled. "You're squishing her!" The little girl pushed away from her mother as she reached underneath her coat.

It looked like a drowned rat, but it was a newborn cat, small and shivering, straining to get closer to the girl's warmth.

Both parents, shaking from fear and relief, now looked closely. The calico kitten was cuddling into the child's neck. Suddenly, it did something amazing.

Below the mustached mouth a tiny tongue flickered over the little girl's eyelid. Stunned, Ava's parents looked at each other in amazement. *Could it be?*

"I told them, Molly," their daughter crooned to the kitten. "Anything can happen at Christmas!"

BARBARA KERNODLE-ALLEN

A CARDINAL AT THE WINDOW

It was almost time for Christmas, but the spirit of the season had not reached Mike and Jenny's house. The stress of building and moving into the new home had taken a toll on their marriage. Everything took longer and cost more than expected. The builders showed up late and took long breaks. Deliveries were often behind schedule. Windows arrived the wrong size. Kitchen tiles were orange instead of the dark red they'd ordered, and replacement tiles were "back ordered." Anticipation turned into exasperation.

The furnace was finally installed on November 30 and the young couple moved into the unfinished house. They decided to live in the house while completing the work that still needed to be done. Mike picked up some overtime to help offset the additional expenses. They felt they could do the painting, install towel racks, crown molding, and wall paper to economize.

Jenny loved their view of snow covered trees, branches hanging low over icy Wills Creek, and their neighbor's old weeping pine, sparkling with ice crystals in the sunlight. But she hated the mess inside the rooms cluttered with drop cloths, paint cans, brushes, tools, and boxes of the things left to be put together and installed. The stink of new wood, carpet, paint, primer, and fresh grout filled the house.

The pressure to get finished before Christmas made it all seem worse. They wanted to be able to decorate and show their new home to family and friends during the holidays, but it wasn't coming together in time. Disappointment eclipsed the joy of the season and the thrill of a new home. Jenny began to complain of headaches. Mike grumbled that his head started to hurt as soon as he entered the front door. They began to avoid each other except when they were working together on a house project. Mike commented that, "Maybe the house wasn't such a good idea right now." Jenny wondered if their marriage was going to survive. She felt sick all the time. All they ever did was work, argue, and complain of headaches.

One cold morning, as she sipped her coffee, Jenny harped, "When are you going to put up the crown molding? I've been tripping over it for weeks. It takes you forever to get things done anymore."

"WHEN I GET TO IT. I have a lot to do. Not that you notice." Mike snapped. "WHAT is that infernal tapping? It's giving me a headache."

Jenny muttered, "Everything gives you a headache. I have one, too. Not that you care."

As the noise became louder, the tapping more insistent, the couple spied the bright crimson plumage of a cardinal perched on the snowy windowsill. The staccato pecking on the window pane threatened to make Mike's head explode.

When Jenny said "Oh, isn't it pretty. It might be hungry. We should feed it. Maybe we should put up a bird feeder," Mike went ballistic. Storming out the French doors to the deck, he yelled, "Feed it? HECK, NO. I'm gonna KILL it!"

Startled by Mike's outburst, disrupting the serenity of the frosty morning, Jim, their new neighbor, looked up from shoveling his driveway in time to see Mike collapse into the snow. Rushing to help the young man, Jim glanced through the open door in time to observe Jenny as she slid from her chair to the floor. A volunteer fireman and EMT, Jim recognized the signs of carbon monoxide poisoning. He dragged Jenny outside, called 911, and started rescue breathing. After assisting the ambulance staff, he called the furnace installer and aired out the house.

The new house didn't get decorated for Christmas that year. There was no tree with lights, no garlands, glass balls, or an angel topper. The crown molding was left on the floor, but the new bird feeder had a lovely wreath.

Jenny said, "We don't need decorations. We have an angel for a neighbor, a cardinal in the yard, and each other."

Mike declared, "I always did love cardinals…almost as much as I love Jenny."

Mike and Jenny share this story with their children every Christmas.

Special Section

DICKENS
VICTORIAN VILLAGE
CAMBRIDGE, OHIO

PAM RITCHEY

THE MAN, THE MARE, AND THE MEMORIES

The chestnut mane of the mare flew with the wind as her graceful legs sped along the path bordering Wills Creek. A middle-aged man, hands scarred from years of hard work, held the reins loosely, enjoying the free-spirited romp of the horse beneath him.

A gentle curve of the creek exposed what he was looking for…a place from time past. With a light tug on the reins, the mare slowed to a trot. Before them lie the burned out remains of a cabin. A towering oak tree, void of leaves in the late December cold, stood guard over scorched timbers of the doorway. Bare saplings and dried stems of various weeds grew where a hard-packed dirt floor once was swept clean.

Dismounting, the man gingerly picked his way through the rubble to a chimney, the only thing left untouched by the blaze. Brushing his hand across the rough stones brought memories of children laughing, small arms bulging from the weight while trying to carry them from the creek bank. He placed them one by one as though putting together a puzzle. The beautiful smile that formed on his young wife's face when it was finally complete was something he'd never forget.

Heavy, wet snowflakes fell from his hat as he shook his head to rouse from the wanderings of his mind. "Come on, Susie. This ain't getting the job done. We have a Christmas tree to find," he said to the mare.

Gathering up the reins, he led her deep within the woods to a grove of pines. Long needles gently swept across the sleeves of his winter coat as he walked from tree to tree, looking for the perfect one.

There it was, about an arm's length taller than his six-foot frame; it stood majestically among the others. Perfectly formed branches gracefully curved upwards from a straight trunk when he shook away the fresh snow.

Carefully binding the branches with rope and attaching it to his saddle horn, he began the long trek home. He led the mare back through the deep woods, waiting to mount until reaching the charred pieces of his former home.

The snow accumulated at a rapid pace, blanketing the ground with four inches in the hour it took him to find the tree. He couldn't afford to spend any more time letting his mind wander through the past. Home was still five miles away, and the going would be slow so as not to damage his special find.

As man and horse walked along, the mare's mane became coated with a thick layer of white, making it impossible to see the rich chestnut hidden underneath. Swirls of mist surrounded them as their warm breath reached the cold evening air. Pulling his hat down tighter on his head, the pair trudged on.

Stars were twinkling in the sky by the time they neared their destination. Smoke from many hearths hung over the village in a thick haze, obscuring the treetops. A soft glow from nearby windows lit the way as they moved through the silent streets.

Rounding a corner, he welcomed the sight of his home. Sweet visions flowed through his mind...neighbors helping raise the new house in town after the old cabin burnt...his lovely wife baking a ham in a range instead of having to do with a fireplace...children, then grandchildren stringing popcorn...stockings hanging on the mantle, waiting to see what Father Christmas may bring.

A young child's face appeared at the front window as the man climbed the few steps of the porch. The door flew open before he made it to the top.

"Grandpa! Did you get our Christmas tree? Where is it? Can we see it now? We have the popcorn all ready!" came the chorus from five youngsters dancing about his legs.

"Now, would I come home without one?" he said.

Squeals of delight echoed through the night as he reached around the side of the house and produced the majestic beauty he had so carefully chosen.

"Oh, Grandpa! It's beautiful!" said the oldest of the group.

"Merry Christmas, Darlin'," he said. As his eyes met those of his wife, he knew...nothing's better than sharing joy with your family at Christmas.

CAREY MOZENA

A LITTLE CHANGE

The warm November sun shone brightly in the park near Wills Creek, but Cindy didn't notice. All she could think about was the fact that Christmas was a month away. Normally, she'd be excited about seeing her kids and grandkids again, whip up a feast, and spend hundreds of dollars on presents.

Not this year.

It wasn't that she didn't want to spend the money; she just didn't have it. One year shy of retirement, she lost her job due to downsizing. All her extra funds went to pay bills while she looked for another job. But who wants to hire an old gramma, anyway?

Despair filled her mind as she wandered around the park. What would her kids think if she didn't cook up a Christmas feast? How would her grandkids react if there weren't dozens of presents to open?

"Hey, Cindy! Watch where you're goin'!" The voice startled her. Looking up, she saw Tami standing in front of her.

"Oh, hi, Tami."

"What's eatin' you?" Tami asked. "Th' sun's shinin', the birds're singin'. It's a beautiful day and you're down in th' dumps. What gives?"

"I got laid off," Cindy told her, "and I can't find another job. I don't know what I'm going to do for Christmas this year. I ain't got the money I used to have."

"So?" Tami smiled. "I never got no money, either. Listen," she took Cindy by the shoulders. "Maybe you're tryin' too hard, y'know? Maybe it's not th' gifts that your family wants. Maybe they'll be just as happy just to spend time with you. Ever think of that?"

"Well..." Cindy thought about it. She always assumed the reason her family loved visiting during the holidays was for the food and presents. She spent money and put on a good show because she worried if she didn't, they'd stop coming.

"Cindy, do what I do," Tami said. "Invite them, but ask that they bring some food. All you do is the turkey, okay?"

"But…,"

"Tut, tut! I wasn't finished. Don't buy any presents either."

"But we've got to have presents!" Cindy protested.

"Make them!" Tami exclaimed. "That's what I do. I never got th' money to buy all those fancy toys anyhow. I sew dolls and quilts and all that. What're you good at?"

"Um…" Cindy couldn't think of anything. "Well, I got a journal," she said meekly.

"A journal, huh?" Tami scrutinized Cindy. "You like to write?"

"Yea." Cindy smiled. "I write everything that happens so I'll always have my memories."

"Of what?"

"Of everything." Cindy thought back to some of her journal entries. "I wrote about when my kids were born, when they got married and had kids of their own, taking them on trips to the pool, the movies, and to the corner store. Not only that…"

"Okay!" Tami interrupted. "Why don't you take those memories an' make stories outta them? Add photos, wrap 'em up, an' have everyone read their story to everybody. Watcha think?"

"They won't want stories," Cindy argued. "The kids'll want toys."

"They already got plenty of toys." Tami looked Cindy in the eye. "Try it. You might be surprised."

The next day, Cindy sent invitations to her kids with a note asking them to bring food. She took out her journal and searched for her favorite memories, working hard over the next month on stories for Christmas. She found ideas in scrapbooking magazines, adding colored paper, ribbons, and beads to the stories. Finally, she placed them on her dining room table by each setting.

Christmas morning, Cindy worried again that her family would be upset at not having a feast or lots of presents waiting for them. However, she composed herself when the doorbell rang. She was surprised that her kids brought several dishes to share—more food and variety than Cindy could have made herself.

Cindy explained that, instead of toys, she wrote everyone a story of a memory past, and then showed them to the table. They spent the rest of the day sharing memories around the Christmas tree.

"Gramma," one of Cindy's youngest grandkids smiled as they were leaving, "this was the bestest Christmas ever."

GRANDPA KEEPS HIS PROMISE

One of the first draftees from nearby Harrison County, Dad was called to serve in World War II. Faith, family, and work were values that were important to him. He had a heart of gold and was always there to help family, friends, or a stranger in need.

In the fall of 1977, we moved to the Wills Valley area. Dad came over to help me house hunt. After looking at several places, we decided on a location overlooking Wills Creek. He drove over on weekends to help us clear the brush and make a path to the creek. He loved that time when the trees were bare. The view across the creek was stunning.

Dad loved holidays, especially Christmastime with family. One year he helped the kids build a model airplane; painted it red, white, and green; and put a motor in it. He'd take the kids out to the Cambridge Airport to fly it. Sometimes they'd go to the airport to watch the planes fly in and out. A fighter pilot in the Army, he never lost his passion for airplanes and telling stories to the kids.

For three years, he came over, walked the path with the kids, and gathered junk with his long-handled metal detector. One day he found an angel clock buried deep under the mud. It was rusty around its metal edges, but all the angels sitting above each number were intact.

"Let's take it back to the house, make it tick. I have some batteries," Grandpa said.

"I don't have a clock. Can I have it for my room?" Joey, his grandson, asked. After trying, they found the batteries didn't work. Grandpa told Joey that he and Grandma would be back for turkey day and they'd get the clock working.

The day before Thanksgiving, Grandpa fell ill and was admitted to the hospital, where numerous tests were run. Family and friends gathered there. Joey ate Thanksgiving dinner with him in his room. "Did that angel clock start to tick?" Grandpa asked.

"Not yet, Grandpa. I'm still waiting," Joey replied.

"When I get well, we'll get it to ticking. Then we'll go out to the airport to watch the planes. I promise."

While driving home from the hospital, the family spotted an airplane circling low overhead. "Grandpa always told us that when a plane flies low an angel is coming to take someone to heaven," Joey said, tears rolling down his cheek before he fell asleep.

A few days before Christmas, Grandpa was still in the hospital. Further testing revealed he had a terminal illness. He looked weaker now. We'd brought him some Christmas packages to unwrap.

Still, he spoke to Joey in a soft whisper. "I'll be up there and we'll get that Angel Clock running." That was the last time we saw him alive.

On Christmas Eve night, we got a call that he quietly passed away a few minutes after midnight. Our Christmas lights still twinkled on the tree and it began to snow. We were doing our best to cope with the situation. Drinking warm milk finally helped us to sleep after the family comforted each other, knowing Jesus called him home to heaven.

Later, the family was awakened when a loud rumble, sounding like thunder, shook the house. The kids ran to the window. "Is it Santa?" cried out Joey's younger brother.

"It's the Angel Pilot. He came to pick up Grandpa and take him to heaven," responded Joey. Knowing how much Grandpa loved to visit the Wills Creek area, he'd have to fly by here one more time.

Until the plane passed over, the family was unable to hear the sound coming from Joey's play tool chest. Apparently, the shaking of the house started the Angel Clock ticking again. Joey ran to his room to get it.

"Grandpa promised he'd have the Angel Clock ticking by Christmas, and he did!" Joey smiled with joy.

LINDA BURRIS

HOLIDAY MEMORIES

During my growing-up years in the late 50's and early 60's, Christmas was a joyful and exciting time. I was the oldest of five children. We lived in a five-room house rented by our parents, which was on a small farm in our community.

My dad worked the swing shift at a tile factory in a nearby city. Mom did housework at home and took in ironing to help Dad with family expenses.

Easter, Thanksgiving, and Christmas were special days. We took part in school and church Christmas programs before Christmas. We children were especially excited when we watched Santa on TV to see if he got our letter. We watched the screen to see if our names were in his big book.

One Christmas morning rule we had to observe was "no getting up before seven." We got out of bed and went to the living room, where the Christmas tree was surrounded by brightly wrapped presents. Any large presents like doll houses, tricycles, or sleds were around the tree too. We received new pajamas, puzzles, board games, a wagon for my brothers, dolls and a new doll house for the girls. There were new jeans, shirts, blouses, underwear, and socks. After opening our presents, we picked up the paper and put it in trash bags. We were certainly blessed and were satisfied as well.

Christmas ended with supper at Grandma and Grandpa Brock's house. We gathered there in the early evening. If everyone in the family was at Grandma's house, the total would be 32. My uncle, aunt, and cousin lived in California and didn't come for either Thanksgiving or Christmas.

Kids and adults were spread out in that five-room house. Supper was at 6:00 p.m. Before opening presents from our grandparents, the dishes were done and put away and the floor swept. We were so full of turkey, potatoes, gravy, green bean casserole, stuffing, homemade rolls, and drinks that some of us had to sit down, be quiet, and allow our food to digest.

Afterwards, we gathered in the living room to unwrap more presents. The carpet was covered with piles of paper and presents. Mom held our gifts while we helped dispose of the holiday debris. At about 9:00 p.m., it was time to go home after a long and busy Christmas day.

When my husband and I had our children, two girls and a boy, we continued to observe some of the same Christmas traditions. On Christmas morning no one was allowed up before 7:00 a.m. We followed the same ritual of opening presents and disposing of paper. In the afternoon, we visited Grandpa Brock, then went to Mom and Dad's house for supper and more presents. Our new traditions included a Christmas Eve service and a visit to Grandpa and Grandma Burris's house for presents and cookies.

Our Christmas now is celebrated differently, since our children have their own homes and holiday traditions. Our daughter, Julie, invites my husband and me to her home before Christmas instead of Christmas Eve, since she and I sing in our church's Christmas Cantata on Christmas Eve. On Christmas afternoon, my husband and I go to my mother's home. Our son, Brian, invites us to his home for lunch on Christmas Day, where we get to see what clothes and toys Santa brought our grandson, Jacob.

The week between Christmas and New Year's Day is also a busy time. As children, we played outdoors; riding sleds, having snowball fights, and playing Follow the Leader along Wills Creek. We also loved making snow angels or a snowman. Cold, wet snow didn't keep us from having fun, especially when some of our friends came to our house. We didn't go into the house until we were cold or it was growing dark.

On New Year's Eve, we piled into the car to drive around our area to see holiday lights. At midnight, we watched the New York City New Year's celebration on television. On New Year's Day we watched the Rose Parade and college football bowl games on TV.

Christmas traditions change over time, but families are still a tradition that will last forever!

EVELYN HILEMAN

DICKENS VILLAGE SURPRISE

The wind was picking up lightweight items, sending them into the air. A discarded plastic bag blew into a tree and caught on a branch. An empty plastic bottle rolled toward Diane. She drew her hood tighter. December is a pretty time of year in Cambridge, Ohio, but wind can make a sunny day icy cold.

Diane lived and worked in Virginia but came to Cambridge to visit her mother. Because she was no longer dating anyone, she often visited her hometown. This was a special trip at Christmastime to enjoy the holidays with her mom. Now was when the downtown was charmingly transformed into an old world England Dickens Village. With the displays of handmade, life-sized mannequins wearing period clothing, Wheeling Avenue was a fun place to be.

Visitors came by cars and buses to see the Dickens scenes. There was also the spectacular Holiday Music Light Show on the Guernsey County Courthouse. Bundled up, visitors strolled the sidewalks taking the self guided tour. A brochure described the lighted Dickens scenes. It all looked so authentic with the historic architecture and antique light posts. Especially with snow.

Diane found an empty bench to sit on and watch the courthouse lights change colors to the beat of music. *It must have been quite an effort to synchronize*, she thought to herself.

Warmer now, she pushed back the hood of her jacket. The wind quickly found her long hair, blowing it about her face.

"Judy? Is that you?" a voice behind her said. Diane didn't reply because she didn't hear. The loud music and the wind whipping her hair prevented it. But the person was closer now, and he spoke loudly, "Judy, is that you?"

Startled, Diane jumped, then pulled her hood up, responding, "No, I am not." She remained on the bench, but when the man came around to face her she began to walk away. *I am NOT Judy, so that's that*, she thought. At a fast pace, she headed to Theo's Restaurant nearby, glad that there were people inside. She felt uncomfortable that this man was following her.

Seeing that there was an empty stool at the counter, she quickly claimed it. But to her consternation the stool beside her became available and HE sat down!

"Miss! Please talk with me. My wife recently died. She had an identical twin but never got to know her before her death. In my grief, I find myself missing Trudy and also looking for her twin. You look so much like her...."

"Well, I am not her. My name is Diane. I don't have a twin."

"Will you at least have lunch with me to talk about it?" he asked.

Just the ploy a serial killer would use, she thought. "I'll have lunch with you on one condition, that my mom joins us!" *That ought to squelch this situation*, she thought.

But he replied, "Oh yes, please do!"

At lunch the next day, they greeted and introduced themselves. As Mark Norman told his story, Diane's mother said the story could be true. The baby she adopted did have an identical twin sister, but the adoption was closed. Her mother thought it best to let life go on with Diane as an only child.

Diane could only gasp, "Oh. Oh!..."

Her mother was stunned too. "Could we meet again—the three of us—and bring pictures and information that could possibly prove this amazing surprise?"

"Oh yes, Mark," Diane implored. "Please bring information. The birth dates are the same!"

Mark pulled out his wallet to show two pictures of Trudy. As Diane passed the pictures to her mother she could hardly speak. It was like looking at herself. Tears formed in the eyes of each of them. What a moment. Then laughter at what this could really mean.

"Yes, let's meet again," said Diane's mother. "Please come for dinner at our house. The Christmas lights on our block are especially pretty this year."

"Yes, please do!" Diane added hopefully.

Mark smiled. "Maybe this won't be the sad, lonely Christmas I expected."

JESUS AND THE KITTEN

Jimmy Callahan, sitting cross-legged on his bedroom floor, nestled the kitten in his arms and kissed it gently on the head. The little orange ball with white feet (thus the name "Sneakers") purred in loving gratitude. Jimmy looked at the poster of Peyton Manning on the wall. *I bet you'd know what to say to them*, he thought.

Mrs. Callahan discovered Sneakers on their front porch in late November. "Poor little thing," she had said. "It can't be much older than five or six weeks. Who would abandon a kitten in this weather?"

Jimmy jumped with delight when his parents agreed that he could keep Sneakers. However, some of the rules pertaining to the kitten seemed grossly unfair to him. First of all, Sneakers did not have free access to all of the house. He was to stay in Jimmy's room, behind a closed door. The kitten seemed happy with the arrangement, as Jimmy provided him with fresh food and water, a clean litter box, toys and scratching posts, and lots of love. But he could not understand why his parents insisted that Sneakers stay in the basement at night. That made no sense at all. It broke his heart to hear muffled "mews" in the middle of the night. He tearfully pleaded with his parents, but was answered with, "Animals shouldn't be in the house" or "That's just the way it is."

"Jimmy," his mother called, knocking on the bedroom door. "We need to leave early in case the roads are bad."

"I'm ready, Mom."

The three climbed into the Subaru and slowly drove down the lane.

"I love church service on Christmas Eve," Mrs. Callahan commented.

"So do I," agreed Mr. Callahan. "After all, this is what Christmas is really about."

Jimmy watched the snowflakes in the car's headlights. *An invading army of millions*, he imagined, *and they've conquered our lane.*

As the car turned from Stone Ridge onto Old Twenty-One Road, a county salt truck passed just ahead of them.

"Thank goodness!" remarked Mrs. Callahan. "I hope he goes all the way to Liberty Methodist."

Reverend Pinter greeted the family as they entered the small country church. "We have a good turnout, considering the weather," he said.

The congregation sang *Joy to the World* and *Silent Night* before the reverend began reading the Christmas story from the Book of Luke.

"And she brought forth her firstborn Son, and wrapped Him in swaddling clothes, and laid Him in a manger, because there was no room for them in the inn."

Mrs. Callahan looked at Jimmy and grinned. He was engrossed with the reading, hanging onto the reverend's every word. *So mature for his nine years*, thought the proud mother.

Some lingered in the parking lot following the service, wishing each other a "Merry Christmas" and exchanging hugs. The snowing had stopped, but not before covering the area in shimmering beauty. The few houses were resplendent with colored lights and other Christmas finery. A steady stream of "oohs" and "aahs" emanated from Mr. and Mrs. Callahan as they drove along Old Twenty-One, but Jimmy remained quietly pensive.

"Don't you like the decorations, Jimmy?" his mother asked.

"They're okay," he answered. "I was just thinking about Sneakers having to stay in the basement."

"Oh, Jimmy!" said his father, rolling his eyes. "We've been through this a hundred times. Animals should not be where people sleep. Do you understand?"

"But Reverend Pinter said tonight that Mary put Baby Jesus in a manger where animals lived. God didn't chase the animals away, but let Jesus sleep among them. If it's okay with God, then why do you think it's wrong?"

Jimmy expected to hear, "Because we said so," or something similar, but his parents were totally silent. *I'd better just keep my mouth shut*, he thought, gazing at the snowy banks of Wills Creek. A deer looked up as they passed.

When they reached Stone Ridge Lane, Mrs. Callahan turned to her son. "Honey, you are absolutely right. Jesus loves all of God's creatures. Even Sneakers."

"No more basement for him," added Mr. Callahan.

"Oh, boy!" Jimmy squealed, clapping his hands, pausing for only a moment to thank the Lord for answering his prayer.

LINDA WARRICK

THE BEST HOLIDAY GIFT

Megan waited patiently in the wheelchair for her mom to bring the car around to the emergency room entrance. Snow mixed with rain was falling softly in tiny little balls, coating the pavement with an icy mix. The volunteer pushing her chair tried hard to lighten the mood. "At least we are not sweltering in the heat," she commented.

"No, but I almost wish we were," replied Megan. "That would mean my husband, Todd, would be home from Afghanistan and our baby would have already been safely delivered."

This was Megan's second trip to the emergency room in the last few months. Her high-risk pregnancy was indeed stressful and the doctor had recommended mostly bed rest. Having her husband halfway around the world was the last thing she needed.

It just didn't seem like it could be Christmas without him. Yes, there was snow, and holiday decorations were everywhere you looked. Her sister, Susan, and family lived out of state and couldn't make it home this year either. So it would be just Megan and Mom on Christmas Eve.

The ultrasound indicated the baby would be a boy and they had already picked out his name, James Tyler Langley. Tyler was for Todd's father and James for her late father. Her father had died in the Vietnam War when she was a toddler. Mom never remarried and had built a successful career in real estate. It was Mom who had been instrumental in helping them find their first home within two miles of her own in the Wills Creek Valley. Megan was forced to move in with her while Todd was away, in case of another medical emergency.

As Christmas approached, she busied herself doing what she could in preparation for the holidays. While crafting some homemade ornaments from the comfort of the sofa, she thought about how Todd loved the Christmas season and all the preparations. He enjoyed stringing up hundreds of lights on their little cabin. There would be none this year. Megan also kept busy sorting through easy recipes to help her mom whip up when she came home from work. Some of her aunts and uncles were coming for dinner Christmas Day.

It was Christmas Eve and, feeling up to it, Megan looked forward to attending Midnight Mass at the local Catholic Church in town. It was a tradition she cherished in celebration of the true meaning of Christmas. There was a beautiful antique Nativity display that seemed to transport everyone who saw it back to Bethlehem. The church sparkled, with thousands of tiny lights adorning the trees and the warm glow of candlelight from the altar and window sills. The pungent aroma of incense intermingled with the pine. The choir sang a selection of traditional hymns that touched her soul, especially her favorite, "Silent Night."

Looking up from her hymn book, she saw a tall figure in a dark uniform moving into her pew. Gasping, she realized that the man was her beloved husband, Todd. Words could not express the astonishment she felt. She sat speechless, overwhelmed as his arms went around her shoulders in a warm embrace. What a surprise! What an unbelievable Christmas this would be. Together they celebrated the true meaning of Christ's coming into the world.

Later that evening, Todd explained that he had been granted a three-week furlough. He was supposed to arrive earlier, but the weather on the East Coast had delayed his flights.

Two weeks later, Megan felt a twinge of pain unlike any she had experienced on the trips she had made to the emergency room. Fearing the worst, Todd quickly whisked her off to the doctor. Yes, it was a little too early, but she was definitely in labor. It seemed little James Tyler Langley was anxious to meet his daddy. Twelve hours later, with Todd by her side, he entered the world, small but in perfect health. It was a holiday neither would forget.

DONNA WELLS

THE BUCKEYE ROOM

Larry happily hummed Christmas carols as he drove to Cambridge. He was headed to his brother's house to spend the holiday. It would also give him a chance to meet his three-week-old niece.

Larry and his brother, Harry, were identical twins. They were exactly alike except for the fact that they had different birthdays. Harry was the oldest, having been born at 11:53 p.m. Larry came into the world 21 minutes later, exactly 14 minutes after the clock struck midnight. Since they each had different birthdays, their mother chose to celebrate Harry's birthday on the 17th of August and Larry's birthday on the 18th of August. Each twin would have a big party on alternating years. The staggered birthdays were probably what set the pattern that would guide them through their entire lives.

Beginning in kindergarten, they refused to dress alike. Each was determined to become his own person. Although there was some sibling rivalry, it was usually good-natured. They loved and respected each other and refused to engage in any serious conflict that would pit one against the other.

By mutual, albeit unspoken, agreement, whenever choices needed to be made, Harry, the oldest, usually picked first. When they played high school football, Harry played offense and Larry defense. Harry was an all-state wide receiver, while Larry was an all-state defensive back. Both boys, being outstanding football players, were aggressively recruited by numerous colleges around the country. However, their dream had always been to play for the Big Ten (plus one), but not at the same school.

Harry picked Ohio State University and Larry went to that school up north, the University of Michigan. Their closeness didn't prevent the friendly rivalry between the brothers as to where their school loyalties lay when it came to the big game.

After the long drive from Ann Arbor and Midnight Mass at St. Benedicts, Larry was exhausted. He fell asleep the minute his head hit the pillow in what Harry referred to as the "Brutus room," so called because of the Ohio State wallpaper, lamps, chairs, bedding, etc. Larry chuckled when he saw the guest room because he had a similar room decorated in maize and blue in his apartment in Michigan.

When Larry awoke, he was drenched in sweat and shocked to see that he was wearing red and gray pajamas. He glanced over at his luggage, stacked in the corner of the room and was surprised to see that it too carried the colors and logo of OSU. He unzipped his suitcase and looked inside. There was a Buckeye hat, scarf, gloves, and socks. He checked his underwear and, sure enough, there was the OSU emblem on a very sensitive spot. His dress shirt was monogrammed with the letters OSU and his tie had a character of Brutus. He thought, *I need some air.*

He dressed quickly and grabbed his jacket which was hanging on a coat tree. Instead of his maize and blue down jacket, there was a red and gray one with the letters OSU on the back. *This must be a joke,* he thought. *My brother is pulling a fast one on me.* "I'm a Wolverine," he said aloud, "I can't be walking around dressed like this." He headed toward his car, parked in the driveway. It too was red and gray with big decals of Brutus on the doors. OSU flags waved from every window.

Just as he turned the key in the ignition, he woke up. "Whew," he said, "that was scary." He headed for the kitchen, where he could smell the coffee and bacon cooking.

When he reached the kitchen, Harry said, "Hi, bro, did you find the guest room comfortable? Hope you had a good night's sleep."

"No way," said Larry, "I just had a horrible nightmare. I dreamt that I was a Buckeye fan and I was headed to Wills Creek dressed in OSU clothing from head to toe."

Harry laughed, "That was a good dream, not a nightmare! GO BUCKS!"

BARBARA KERNODLE-ALLEN

MITTENS' NEW LIFE

Half-grown Mittens lived with his human, Mary, who kept his black and white coat brushed and his dishes filled. He lived a pampered life, snoozing by a sunlit window in the little house in Kimbolton. There were bugs, rodents, and frogs to chase along the banks of Wills Creek at night. Frisky, playful Mittens was a happy kitty.

Then, Guy, Mary's new boyfriend, moved in. Pretending to like Mittens, he tormented the poor cat when Mary wasn't looking. Jealous of the attention Mary lavished on her pet, Guy planned to dispose of his feline rival. Mittens hid behind the sofa when Guy was home.

One December evening, while Mary was Christmas shopping, Guy put Mittens in a burlap bag.

"You're going for a ride, cat. And you're not coming back."

Guy sped down Old 21 Road and tossed the bag with Mittens in it out the car window into a snow bank across from the Guernsey Psychiatric Hospital. He let Mary think the cat had just wandered off.

Frightened and disoriented, Mittens clawed and fought his way out of the bag. He scrambled to the top of the mound of ice and snow and looked around. A hostile yowl from the nearby horse barn told him a newcomer would not be welcome. Mittens headed across the road toward the sprawling brick buildings of the psychiatric hospital. He smelled heat and food. The faint sounds of human voices were reassuring to the cold, wet cat.

Edna, a shift supervisor, stood outside the hallway door. The frigid air was a relief from the overheated hospital. Thinking about retirement, and trying to avoid thinking about the lonely Christmas ahead, she took a long drag on her cigarette. Sounds coming from the holiday party in the gym made her feel even sadder. Her son, her only child, couldn't get away from his new job at the computer company in Georgia this year. It wouldn't be Christmas without him. She closed her eyes, leaned back against the cold brick wall, and sighed.

Startled by an unfamiliar sound, Edna peered into the dark shadows surrounding the building. What was it? Raccoon? Skunk? Fox? Maybe a deer come up to lick salt from the icy walkways. She reached for the door.

The human was going to get away. Picking up all the speed he could muster, Mittens let out a desperate "MEOW" as he floundered toward her through the snow.

Seeing the miserable little cat struggling to reach her touched Edna's heart. This little mite needed help.

"Oh, kitty, where did you come from?"

Edna took off her sweater and, scooping Mittens up, she wrapped him in the warm cardigan. "You poor little thing. You're all wet. Let me dry you off."

Cuddling the kitty in the sweater, Edna smuggled him down the hallway to her office. Purring filled the supervisor's office when she offered Mittens some tuna from her sandwich.

"What's your name, boy?"

Mittens just purred and rubbed his chin on her shoe.

"Aren't you sweet?"

Mittens jumped in Edna's lap and fell asleep.

Next morning, Edna placed the little stray in a box in her car. On the way home, they stopped at the grocery store for cat food and kitty litter. She forgot her loneliness, enjoying her new pet.

"This isn't going to be such a bad Christmas after all."

Mittens purred.

Once in Edna's house, with a full tummy, Mittens began to play. He skittered across the vinyl kitchen floor, dancing through the rooms chasing his tail and jumping on furniture. An old Fred Astaire/Ginger Rogers movie was on TV.

"You look like Fred Astaire in that tuxedo coat of yours. I think I'll call you Fred." Edna laughed.

In his new home, Mittens, now known as Fred, spends his days snoozing in Edna's sunny window. Chitter-chattering at the birds and squirrels in the neighbor's peach tree, he watches people come and go in the accounting office parking lot behind Edna's house. At night, he hides beneath the lilac, stalking bugs and rodents. There are no frogs or creek in Fred's new life, but he doesn't miss them.

ANNUAL TREE BATTLE

If you want a Christmas tree, get it yourself," shouted Gary. "I get tired of taking the tree out of the box every year and putting it together."

"Where did you kids put the star for the top of the tree?" asked Melinda. "It should be in that box somewhere."

Busy playing their video games after ice skating on Wills Creek, the children appeared too tired to help. "Jacob and I will help decorate when we are finished with our games," Sarah promised.

Sitting in her rocking chair, Granny watched and listened to the family arguing about putting up the Christmas tree. This happened every year, taking a lot of the Spirit of Christmas out of the season in Granny's opinion.

As she rocked, she thought back to a Christmas long ago when she was a little girl. They always enjoyed the beauty of Christmas during the bleak winter months.

Dad smiled while he exclaimed with a twinkle in his eye, "Hop in the pickup. We are going for a ride in the country."

"Where are you taking me?" asked little Annie while bouncing up and down.

"It will be a surprise!"

So off they went down Hopewell Hill and across Indian Camp Run Road to a hill of pine trees owned by the Ross family. Now Annie smiled from ear to ear, since the Christmas tree was her favorite part of the season. She just loved helping her Dad pick out their Christmas tree.

They would walk over the steep hillside until Annie found the perfect tree. Dad never complained! He would saw it down and carry it carefully to the back of the pickup. They gave the Ross family a dollar for the tree but it seemed well worth it to Annie.

Back home, Annie loved to help decorate the tree. Dad would put it in the stand and Mom would always put on the lights, as she knew Annie couldn't reach very high. These lights with big colored bulbs lit up the whole room. A pine smell drifted through the house. You could smell it when you opened the front door.

Annie helped put on their few special glass ornaments very gently so she didn't break any. Then they would make popcorn to string with a needle and thread to wrap around the tree. Oh, how pretty it looked! Many strands of popcorn appeared white as snow on the tree.

Red and gold ribbons looked beautiful on the branches. They also had a package of icicles that they bought at Newberry's for a dime. Annie put them on one icicle at a time. When the icicles caught the lights of the tree, they glowed with rainbows of colors.

Granny shook her head and came back to the present, where she heard the family still complaining about the difficulties of putting up the Christmas tree. They were missing so much by using a tree from a box instead of a fresh cut tree, especially for the wonderful pine smell. And the lights were all white and already on the branches. Granny liked pretty colors to brighten the night. Most of all, she missed that happy Spirit of Christmas.

Later that evening, when they went to Mantua Methodist Church to practice for the Christmas program, the decorated tree stood by the altar. Live trees, now considered a fire hazard, no longer appeared in public buildings. But the tree was still beautiful with ornaments of red and gold.

Jacob watched with big eyes while they lit the tall tree. At the age of four, he was excited to have a tree in the church. Jacob looked at his Mom and said, "It looks like a big birthday cake for Jesus!"

Mom's heart skipped a beat as she realized the significance of the tree to the children. When they returned home, the Christmas tree decorating took on a new spirit. They even sang "It's Beginning to Look a Lot Like Christmas" while putting on the candy canes.

Granny sat in her rocker and smiled a big smile. She thought the Christmas tree did look like a big birthday cake for Jesus.

DONA McCONNELL

MIRROR IMAGE

Miranda took her place in line, a familiar ritual at the orphanage. The children lined up by height, like the wooden soldiers on the shelves at Henry's toy store. Miranda wore her only dress, a dreary cast-off, like the girl herself. Everyone stood perfectly still, barely breathing as they waited for the visitors.

"Choosers," the older kids nicknamed the smiling couples coming to select a new son or daughter. Miranda, now ten, had been seven when her caseworker dropped her at the Wills Creek Children's Home, terrified and lonely.

Fear turned to joy when she discovered visiting days. Finally, she'd have a home!

But now those days were the worst of all. Couples wanted babies. The really pretty girls had a chance, but Miranda knew she didn't fit that category.

"Poor child," she heard one floor mother whisper to the headmaster as the children decorated the Christmas tree with popcorn and pinecones. "So plain, with her pale skin and mousy brown hair. We'll never get rid of her." Miranda felt her heart break, then harden to stone. "Never" rang in her ears like one sour note in a beautiful symphony. The bushy tree now looked like a pathetic symbol of joy and merriment in a place with neither.

There were two couples. One was young and blond with dazzling movie star smiles. The other was an older, faded version of the first. When the golden couple chose a baby from the crib section, Miranda nearly gasped with relief.

The older couple was just turning from Jason, the twelve-year-old to her left. ("Unadoptable due to age," his chart said.) The woman wasn't attractive, but her pleasant smile made her ordinariness less noticeable. Stopping at Miranda, the woman's expression changed. She and her husband exchanged startled glances. The woman turned back to the young girl and did something unexpected—she laughed.

Though soft and musical, the laugh struck Miranda like a physical blow. She stumbled backward and, burning with shame, bolted down the hall and through the outside door. She hadn't cried in years, yet tears were dripping onto her ragged dress.

The couple caught up with her as she collapsed under a tree. Tentatively, the woman reached out, touching her arm. "Oh, child, did we scare you? Why did you run away?"

Still sobbing, Miranda could only squeak. "Funny," she said. The woman's confused face suddenly registered pain.

"Funny? Oh, Frank, she thought we were laughing at her." She began to gently wipe Miranda's tears with the tail of her dress.

"Tell her about the picture, Stella," Frank said, pushing up wire spectacles that framed kind eyes.

"Frank means the picture in our living room, dear," the woman said. "It's a picture of me with my mother. She died when I was quite young. It's my most treasured possession."

Miranda understood loss, but what did this have to do with her?

"We've gone to orphanages for years looking for the right child, but always left feeling sad. I was ready to give up, but Frank wanted to try one more time."

"When I saw you, after so many years of disappointment, I laughed with joy." Stella's voice filled with emotion. Frank continued as he patted his wife's back.

"You look exactly like the girl in the picture, Miranda—like Stella when she was your age."

"I suddenly knew what I'd been looking for," Stella said. "A child who looked like she belonged with us." The tearful child stared in disbelief.

"Do you think you might give us another chance? We don't have much, but we have lots of love to give to a special little girl like you," Stella continued.

Miranda's arms reached toward Stella, who scooped her up and hugged her tightly. Frank and Stella laughed as their new daughter began to cry again, tears of joy for the couple who thought she—plain, mousy Miranda—was special.

Miranda saw the other children peeking through the window by the shabby tree, which now looked like the grandest, most beautiful Christmas tree in the world.

PEACE AND HARMONY

It came to pass that all the lesser animals from the forest had a meeting under the Big Pine Tree down by Wills Creek. Attendees included Chippy, the chipmunk; Hippity, the rabbit; Jake, the turkey; Chitter, the red squirrel; Chatter, the gray squirrel; Woody, the red-headed woodpecker; and other assorted feathered and furry friends. The meeting was presided over by Hoot, the wise old owl.

Hoot called the meeting to order and asked the reason for the meeting. Chitter and Chatter both tried to talk at once and nobody could understand a word either said. Hoot held up his wings to stop them both and called on Hippity.

Hippity hopped up on the speaking rock and said, "Wiley Coyote and Robert Bobcat do not have enough of the Christmas Spirit."

Chitter and Chatter in unison echoed his words, "Definitely not enough spirit."

Hoot glared at the two squirrels and said, "You two keep quiet. Hippity has the rock. Let him speak for himself. Now, Hippity, why do you say they don't have the Christmas Spirit?"

Hippity took a deep breath and said, "Well, Sir, as we all know, during the Christmas season there is a truce among all the forest animals. For a week before and a week after Christmas, all the animals in the forest must control their appetites and tempers so everyone can celebrate the birth of the Christ Child in peace and harmony. Well, just this week, Wiley tried to catch me twice in one day, and yesterday Robert was seen slinking around trying to get close to Jake. This is in direct violation of the Christmas Spirit Rules. Something has to be done about them." His remarks finished, Hippity hopped off the speaking stone.

Woody glided up on top of the speaking stone, tapped it several times with his beak to clear his throat, and said, "I was up in that old elm tree by the bend in Wills Creek and saw the whole thing. *Tap, tap, tap*. Yes, I saw those two bah-humbugs try to catch Hippity and Jake. *Tap, tap, tap*."

Chippy hopped up on the stone, flipped his tail several times, and said, "The question is, what are we going to do with these two culprits? Christmas just won't be the same if we can't celebrate it in peace and harmony." Chippy flitted off the stone.

Hoot flapped his wings for order and asked, "Does anyone have a suggestion? What can we do about these rascals?"

Everyone had an idea but, unfortunately, nobody would listen to anyone else's idea. For a time there was just a bedlam of voices, each trying to be louder than the next and nothing was getting done. Hoot had to flap his wings for several minutes before order was restored.

When Hoot got them quieted down, Ricky Raccoon daintily walked up and sat on the stone and said, "I suggest we simply tell them to behave or they won't get invited to the Christmas party. I mean, it is the biggest event of our year and everybody wants to be there."

Hoot immediately said, "We have a suggestion to ban them from the Christmas party if they don't follow the rules. Those in favor hold up your paw, or wing, as the case may be."

Everyone raised one or more digits to make sure they got counted. "How many opposed?" Not one paw or wing went up. "The ayes have it. Now who is going to tell them about our decision?"

Everyone paused and looked at each other. No one wanted to be the one that had to talk to Wiley Coyote or Robert Bobcat. That could get ugly in a hurry if either of them decided to ignore the warning.

Hoot looked around at the others and asked for volunteers. Not one member would step forward to take up the dangerous task. With a mournful "Hoot, hoot," he sighed, "I guess I'll have to be the one to deliver the message. Hoot."

And so it came to pass that the animals in the forest had a very Merry Christmas after all.

OLD MAN WINTERS

Old Man Winters had a sour disposition. His attitude was as cold as his name. He was known as "Scrooge" to everyone in Wills Creek. Bent with age, Old Man Winters frowned at everyone as he hobbled past. After being "Bah, humbugged" again, Mark decided it was time to sweeten the old man. Gathering at the playground, Mark called a meeting of all the children in the area.

"Alright," Mark said. "We all know why we're here, right?" Five heads nodded at him. "Any idea why Scrooge hates Christmas?"

"I'll bet he hates roasted chestnuts," a rotund boy said.

"Maybe he's a vegetarian and doesn't like all those turkeys and gooses being cooked," a small girl piped up in back.

"It's 'geese', not 'gooses', dipstick," a boy with a baseball cap retorted.

"Back to the point!" Mark said. "Any other ideas?"

"D'you think he gets any presents?" a little boy asked.

"That's gotta be it!" Mark exclaimed. "Scrooge hates Christmas because he never gets presents!"

"We could get him a new bicycle," the little boy said. "I've always wanted one."

"Adults don't want bicycles, moron," Baseball Cap said. "He'd want a car."

"We don't have money for a car," Mark said. "Besides, Pa says he's already got more cars than he needs. Any other ideas?"

"How about a ball and glove?" another boy asked. "I love playing baseball with my pa."

"A book?" a redheaded girl suggested. "I like curling up with a good book."

"That's stupid," Baseball Cap spoke up. "Reading's lame-o."

"Says you!" the redheaded girl argued. "You probably can't read anyway!"

"I can too read!"

"Stop it, you two!" Mark jumped between them. "Fighting isn't gonna help Scrooge. Now focus!" The two gave up and Mark sat back down.

"Hey, guys," the rotund boy said, "I gotta go home for dinner."

"Me, too," the little girl said.

"Alright," Mark sighed. "Meeting adjourned. See you later." They mumbled goodbyes as they parted ways.

The next day, Mark browsed the internet looking for anything about Old Man Winters and what he might like for Christmas. He stumbled upon an old newspaper article about a fire at the Winters' mansion over 60 years ago. The article said the fire started when the Christmas tree caught fire overnight. Winters managed to escape, but his wife and child didn't. There was a picture of a beautiful young woman holding an infant with the article.

The children had agreed to meet on Christmas Eve to go to Old Man Winters' house to deliver their gifts. Each one had a present for him. Baseball Cap bragged about how his was better than all the others, but he fell silent as they approached Old Man Winters' house.

"Go ahead, Mark," Baseball Cap whispered. "Knock on the door."

Just then the door flew open and the bent figure of Old Man Winters stood over them.

"What are you doing on my doorstep?" he cried. "No children allowed!"

"M-Merry Christmas, Mr. Winters," Mark stammered. The old man stared at him.

"Merry Christmas!" the other children said as they held out their gifts.

"Land sakes!" he said. "Are all those gifts for me?"

"Yes, sir!" Mark said.

"Well, I'll be!" Old Man Winters shook his head and stepped back. "Come in, children. Come in!" He led them inside to a huge sitting room.

The children watched Old Man Winters open their gifts. Mark gave his gift last. It was a collage of the pictures he found online of Old Man Winters and his family. He saw a tear in the old man's eye when he opened it.

"How did you know?" Old Man Winters whispered as he stared at the pictures.

"I'm sorry you lost your family in that fire, Mr. Winters, but I don't think they'd want you to stop celebrating Christmas, or be angry with everyone. They'd want you to have a Merry Christmas, too."

THE TRAIN TRIP TO LAZARUS

It is early in the morning when we arrive at the Cambridge train station. My aunts have decided I should experience a train trip, so we are going to the big city of Columbus, Christmas shopping. This was in the early 1940's. I was four or five years old.

As the train slowed to a stop at the station, there was a lot of hissing and clanging. The engineer blew the whistle while steam poured out around the engine. The porter checked our tickets and placed a stool on the platform for us to use as a step to the passenger car.

We were the McBride's: Grandma, Dad's sister Margaret, his Aunt Pauline, Mother, her sister, Margaret Lanning, and me, Hattie.

The train started out very slowly. Soon we were crossing Wills Creek, then into the tunnel and out the other side, all the while picking up speed. Soon the whistle was blowing for Frazier's crossing and there was our farm. What a thrill to see our barn and house fly by, for I had grown up watching the trains pass our house several times a day. Now, here I am on a train. Aunt Margaret McBride was taking me on a train tour, explaining everything as we went. In the dining car, she treated me to hot chocolate and toast.

Arriving in Columbus, we caught a streetcar downtown to the Lazarus Department Store on High Street. This was my first time to see its animated Christmas window. I could have watched the beautiful scenes all day but the aunts were off to shop. We headed inside, where everything was a'bustle with beautiful Christmas decorations everywhere. I loved it. As I clutched for dear life onto Aunt Pauline's fur coat, we buzzed by the jewelry and perfumes to the bank of elevators, where we were zipped up to the children's floor. Here, they had made a small North Pole setting in the back of the store. Santa was seated high on a throne.

The excitement of seeing Santa was almost more than I could

stand. Mother and Aunt Margaret Lanning and I waited in line forever before an elf came out with a sign that said, "Santa is feeding his reindeer." *Wow! Reindeer, wonder where they might be?* I thought, *They're up on the roof!* I wanted to watch Santa feed his reindeer, but instead we went to lunch at Mill's Cafeteria. I don't remember what I had to eat, but I was astounded at all the food choices.

Tall, skinny Grandma McBride watched me stare wide-eyed at her three pieces of pie and told me only adults could do this, but did she did share with me.

Finally we were back at Lazarus, waiting again in line to see Santa. Looking around the store, I was so fascinated with all the beautiful things. The toys were out of this world. The dollies were so beautiful! How I loved the trains! Because I was a girl I never got a train, but I loved to watch them run around the tracks through the tunnels, blowing the whistle, with real steam coming out of the engine. I knew in my heart "trains are only for boys" was not right.

Finally, it was my turn to talk to Santa. He was so beautiful, but I was tongue-tied and could only shake my head. Mother was upset that I didn't tell him what I wanted for Christmas, but the aunts assured me he would know what I wanted. I hung on to the candy cane he gave me all the way home.

All I remember about the train ride home was pulling into the Cambridge train station and there was my Daddy, Grandpa, and Uncle Ramsey waiting for us. What a day!

Christmas at Lazarus became a tradition for my family. Children and grandchildren were treated each year to all its splendor. The trips ended only when Lazarus closed its doors and the Christmas wonderland was no more.

JOETTA VARANASI

SOLVING A HOLIDAY MYSTERY

During the weekend before Thanksgiving, the weather was like spring in East Cambridge. Joe was outside hanging Christmas lights. His older kids were married and had moved away. They came home for Thanksgiving, but spent Christmas in their own homes. Joe and Mary enjoyed Christmas with Joey Jr., their youngest son, who lived at home.

Mary was busy decorating the tree. Boxes of ornaments sat on the floor. An aroma of chocolate chip cookies wafted from the oven. Pine scent from the freshly cut tree penetrated the house. She wondered, *Should I use the wreaths and Santa, or the turkeys and cornstalks?* The beautiful horn of plenty centerpiece that Gina, her daughter, had made in high school would have to blend with Santa, snowmen, wreathes, bells, and a manger under the tree.

Pulling out old ornaments, Mary found a metal reindeer engraved with "Merry Christmas 1973." It also bore her first son's name, Frank. She hung Baby's First Christmas bulbs, in red glitter with names of her twin daughters, Tina and Gina, then angel ornaments with Mary and Joe's names painted in silver. The twins had made them in catechism class. Then she placed St. Anthony, patron saint of lost items, beneath the tree next to the manger. Memories of past Christmases flashed through her mind.

When Joey Jr. was ten, his favorite Christmas ornament disappeared. He had made it in kindergarten and loved it very much. It was a wooden airplane painted red, white, and green. His name was engraved on one of the wings. The plane had always been the largest ornament on the tree. How it got lost remained a mystery.

Mary was deep in thought when Joe entered. "Oh!" she said, "I was thinking of Joey's airplane and how it hung in the middle of our tree. The kids thought Santa took it in exchange for their gifts."

"I remember that Christmas morning like yesterday," Joe answered in a soft voice. "We went out and checked Bruno's doghouse, then looked around the yard to see if he carried it off. We asked neighbors if the cat had dragged anything into their yards. Checked all garbage bags with Christmas wraps, but no luck."

Three days before the family was to come home for Thanksgiving, it began to rain. Wills Creek was flooding. They made it home safely with their families just in time to help clean up two feet of water in the basement. Following the flash floods, East Cambridge was crippled with a water break.

Frankie and Joe were outside cleaning up the mess from the flood waters. "I don't believe it!" yelled Frankie. "I can't believe what I'm seeing!" He bent down to pick up a warped-wood, four-inch object with wings. The paint had long since worn off, but the engraved name, "Joey," was still visible.

"It's been ten years since this ornament was lost!" cried Joey. "Why couldn't we find it before?"

Obviously, the flash flood waters unraveled dirt and debris that hadn't been moved in years, washing it into the backyard. Joey was reunited with his favorite ornament.

After dinner, the family opened gifts, later talking about the night the airplane ornament disappeared. Joey said he would repaint it and hang it on the tree once again.

Tina spoke up. "I have a confession. I got up that night to see if Santa had come. Bruno had the airplane in his mouth. I grabbed it and placed it back on the tree, but Bruno must have taken it off again. I didn't tell anyone because we'd received complaints about Bruno bothering things in the neighborhood. I was afraid we'd have to give him away. Sorry."

"Let's all sing Christmas carols. It's a small miracle that Joey's airplane came home for Christmas," Mary said in a joyful voice.

Joey and Frankie grabbed their guitars. The twins sat at the piano and everyone sang "Oh, Christmas Tree."

Mary placed the airplane in the middle of the tree. Joey would refinish it tomorrow.

SAMUEL D. BESKET

A Present from the Past

Gene reluctantly turned into the driveway of his mother's home. He couldn't believe it'd been six months since her passing. *One day she was raking leaves and the next she…….well,* he thought, *the new owners want to move in before Christmas, so I better get this done. This would be easier if my wife, Rhonda, was here. But she recently deployed to Iraq with her medical squadron. I'll be spending the holidays by myself.*

Unlocking the back door, Gene walked into the kitchen. Sitting down at the old white table, he looked at the worn spot in the middle. Running his hand over it, he could still picture his mom rolling out cookie dough.

Moving through the house, he quickly placed tags on some of her furniture. Most of the stuff would be taken to the Wills Creek Auction House. He wanted to save but few pieces for nostalgic reasons.

The next few hours passed in a blur as he agonized over various pieces of furniture. *We can't keep it all,* he thought. Finally, everything was tagged except the dining room set, and there were a few closets yet to clean out.

Looking at the table brought back memories of family dinners. *Mom always set a plate for everyone, he thought, even when we were in the service. It was her way of remembering us.*

Going through the various closets made Gene think about how little his parents had. Hardly a plate or coffee cup matched; many had small chips and cracks. But they never complained.

Opening the door to a large closet in his parents' bedroom, Gene sorted through boxes of old Christmas lights, greeting cards, and wrapping paper. Dragging an old weathered cardboard box out into the room, he dusted off the top. As he read the faded letters, he gasped at what he saw.

"American Flyer," he shouted. "My train. I...thought this was gone." Gently, he opened the yellowed box, revealing the blue train engine. *I can't believe this*, he thought. *I can't believe it's still here. It's not lost.*

Glancing at his watch, Gene did some quick calculations. Fourteen hour time difference between here and Iraq. That meant he could call Rhonda in about two hours. She would be as surprised as he was when he told her about the train.

The last item in the closet was his mom's old aluminum Christmas tree. Slowly, he removed the pole and branches. Gently placing them in the predrilled holes, he plugged in the color wheel. The room was immediately transformed into an array of red, green, and blue colors.

Dialing the eleven-digit number, he waited until the overseas operator came on line before entering Rhonda's personal number.

"Hello."

"Rhonda, is that you?" Gene asked. "Your voice sounds garbled."

"It's me, Gene, we're having a sandstorm. Is everything okay?"

"You won't believe what I found in Mom's house.... remember that blue electric train I told you I had as a boy? I found it in a closet, along with Mom's old aluminum Christmas tree. It's all here and they both work."

"That's great, Gene. What do you plan on doing with it?"

"I've thought about this for the last few hours and I think I've found the perfect place for it."

After the short call, Gene busied himself with last minute shopping. He finally had time to relax on Christmas Eve. The large Christmas tree in the corner of his living room cast a warm feeling over the room. Dozing off momentarily, he was startled by the ringing of the phone.

"Mr. Hanes, this is Richard Alexander. My wife and I recently bought your mother's house."

"Yes," Gene replied, "Is everything okay?"

"More than okay, sir. With all the expenses of moving, we didn't have much money left to buy Christmas for the boys. When they walked into the house and saw the tree with the train around it they were ecstatic. What a blessing it was for the boys. Hope you have a very Merry Christmas, sir. May God bless you."

"He already has," Gene replied. "He already has."

LINDA BURRIS

THE CHRISTMAS ANGEL

Jane Martin, 34, and nine months pregnant, looked out the living room window where soft, fluffy snowflakes were falling. They had been pelting the ground for the last hour. The crystals picked up the beautiful reflection from the neighbor's Nativity scene across the street. Four inches of snow covered the ground.

She could hear "Silent Night" coming from the magnificently decorated United Methodist steeple on the hill to the west. Dan, her husband, a nurse at Grant West, called, telling her he would be home as soon as his shift was over at 11:00 p.m.

Jane was watching the Christmas scene being played when the pains began. "Oh, no," she cried. She had hoped she would have their baby before Christmas. She was having another sharp pain when the cell phone rang. "What's wrong? asked her mother.

"I'm having my baby!" Jane wailed.

"Goodness gracious," said her anxious mother. "How close are the pains?"

"About three minutes apart. How am I going to get to the hospital with all this snow? The streets are covered. It's only 9:00 p.m. Dan won't be home until 11:30. Help me, Mom!"

"I can't do anything but call 9-1-1 and have an ambulance sent."

"Okay, Mom! I'll pray that they get here before the baby comes. I'll call Dan at the hospital."

As she hung up, the doorbell rang. Jane looked out to see their neighbor, John Cable, standing on the porch. She turned on the porch light and let him in. John said, "Need your sidewalk shoveled?"

"No," said Jane. "Would you like some coffee while you get warm?"

John, 64, dressed in coveralls and boots, entered the foyer, looked at Jane, and exclaimed, "Jane, you're pale. Are you okay?"

"I'm in labor. The baby isn't due for two weeks. How am I going to get to the hospital in time? My mom is calling 9-1-1 for me, and Dan is working until 11:00. I feel another pain coming. Hurry, help me!"

John quickly helped Jane prepare for delivery, collecting scissors, string, hot water, towels, and blankets. He was ready and so was the baby. In three minutes, baby Virginia uttered a shrill cry. John tied the umbilical cord with the string and cut it. He wrapped her in a towel, cleaned her, then gently handed her to Jane.

Before the ambulance arrived, Jane said, "I prayed for help and you came. You're Virginia's Christmas angel!"

"Yes! I will be Virginia's Christmas angel," John said, gazing at the beautiful miracle in her mother's arms.

WHO WAS THERE?

Who was there on that Holy Night so long ago?

Shepherds were there to see the baby in the stable.

Who was lying in a manger?

Jesus, God in the flesh, was lying in a manger bed of hay.

Who was watching over his sleeping?

Mary and Joseph were watching over the sleeping baby.

Who was singing in the skies above?

Angels were singing praises to the newborn king.

What was shining in the sky?

A star was shining brilliantly over the stable in Bethlehem.

Who stood around the bed of hay?

The cows, sheep, and donkeys beheld the sleeping child.

Why did he come?

He came to save a lost and dying world.

What did he come to do?

Redeeming work to save mankind.

For whom?

For you and me.

JENNA'S GIFT

"Hurry!" Jenna squealed as I carefully picked open the package. "I can't wait for you to see what I got you." She grinned that exquisitely silly excited grin that only Jenna could pull off without looking like a fool.

It was Christmas morning in 1963, when I was almost eleven years old and Jenna was fifteen. We were close despite our age difference. My vivacious, pretty brunette older sister had sparkling brown eyes and a heart as big as the Guernsey County farm we grew up on. I was going through that awkward ugly duckling stage of life, a tomboy who loved working on our Wills Creek family farm. My burnished blonde hair was more likely to be blown by the wind than sleekly coiffed like Jenna's, but I adored her and she doted on me.

Briefly, I dragged out the unwrapping process, just to drive her crazy, but her excitement overrode my youthful tendency to tease. Shredding quickly the last layer of paper, I peeled away clinging vestiges of tissue like last summer's sunburn. As I turned the box right side up, my mouth dropped open. "Oh, Jenna! How did you…" My voice trailed off into an ecstatic squeal as I jumped to my feet to hug her fiercely, my eyes already pooling with tears.

It was a beautiful pink Barbie and Ken trunk. Inside was a blonde Bubblecut Barbie wearing a delicate pink strapless satin gown, a white fur stole, and long white gloves. Around her neck, a triple strand pearl choker with drop pearls set off the outfit. She wore matching pearl drop earrings. She was beautiful. Beside her, a handsome blonde tuxedoed Ken sported a burgundy cummerbund with matching bowtie. Jenna and I had seen this very Barbie and Ken on Saturday morning commercials, but I never thought I'd have one of my own. From that moment on, I dreamed of being like Barbie.

"Whatcha got there?"Dad grinned as he bent over me to see the object of my delight. "Ooh, she's a beauty all right. Jenna, you must've babysat the Perkins' kids for months to earn the money for this."

Jenna just smiled that brilliant white smile of hers, thoroughly enjoying my happiness at her gift.

Mamma raised her eyebrows a little. "I wonder if it isn't a little too sophisticated for you, Barbara. Very lovely, but somewhat adult for a girl your age. Don't you agree, Robert?"

My eyes flew to my father's face. *Please don't say yes, Daddy. Please don't say yes*, my heart cried out. I think he heard it, or read it in my eyes, because he said, "Well, Darling, I don't see how we can ask Barbara to part with it now, do you? Besides, I know she'll take especially good care of it, knowing how dear a gift it was for Jenna to give."

I hugged the trunk to my chest, my eyes overflowing with joy and love for my father. "Oh, Jenna, this is the best gift ever. I'll take very good care of it, I promise. You worked so hard to get it for me. "

Mamma clucked her tongue and shook her head, smiling demurely, acquiescing to my father's benevolence. "I'm sure you're right, Robert."

My gift to Jenna that year paled in comparison, but she vowed her love for the delicate bracelet Mamma had helped me choose. I paid for it with pin money from doing extra chores in the house. "It's beautiful, Barbara—just like you," Jenna cooed as she hugged me close.

Remembering that special Christmas gift always brings tears to my eyes. Jenna passed away a few months later of appendicitis. We laid her to rest in the family cemetery with the delicate bracelet on her arm. My heart went with her as well.

My father tells me I've grown into a lovely young woman, so much like the older sister I adored. I still keep my promise to Jenna. Only on special occasions do I lift the beautiful dolls carefully out of their trunk. Instead, I display them in my bedroom where I gaze at them every day, caressing the soft satin skirt of Barbie's gown from time to time, remembering my sister's love for me.

WILLS CREEK CEMETERY SURPRISE

"Dad! Guess what I found today!" Tyler asked.

"What's that?" his father replied, never taking his eyes off the newspaper he was reading.

"I found our last name on a tombstone! I was with the Boy Scouts."

"Was it spelled the way we spell our name?"

"It sure was!"

"We've lived here for years and I've never known anyone with our last name. What cemetery were you in and why at Christmastime?" his father asked as he continued to read.

"The old Wills Creek Cemetery. The scoutmaster asked if anyone wanted to earn points toward their community service award. We had to sweep snow away from the tombstones so there wouldn't be so much water near the graves; the ground there has deteriorated. We also set up headstones that had fallen over. No one visits that cemetery anymore," Tyler replied.

His dad said nothing, but Tyler tried again. "That's not all I found!"

"That's nice, Tyler," was his dad's answer.

"I'm bothering you...never mind..." Tyler turned to leave, but his mother, Kate, entered the room.

"Lloyd, talk with your son. He wants to tell you something and you hardly pay attention. One day, he won't even try to communicate with you."

"Oh, all right!" The newspaper came crashing down. "What else, Tyler?"

"I found a coin..." He didn't put his hand out. He never knew how his dad would act. It was often a tense time talking with him. He felt closer to his mother, who was always interested in his activities. It was easier to just avoid his dad.

"Let's see the coin. Hey, this looks like solid gold! Where did you find it?" His dad was interested now.

"At the base of the headstone with our same name on it. I wanted to do an extra good job at that headstone so when I brushed hard, I saw something shiny. I used the broom handle to dig it up."

Tyler's Dad smiled. "Show us where this was."

Soon they were at the headstone in the old cemetery. The name was so worn only the last name showed distinctly. Was the first name Martha? Margaret? Hard to tell. The date was a faint 18, probably 1800's.

"Wish we could learn something about this person..." Lloyd said. "I'll dig around the base to see if there's anything else."

There was! A small leather pouch with a glass vial inside. "Oh, open it!" Kate exclaimed. "Looks like a note in there!"

"We'll open it at home," Lloyd overruled.

Back at the house, heating cocoa, Kate wondered, *What could possibly be inside?*

Lloyd removed the leather pouch from his handkerchief. The vial's cork stopper crumbled with age but the note was readable. Some words were misspelled. The note read:

"I was just a lad when pa died, and ma, having no money, knew we had to return to Guernsey County where family could hep us. But it was a long ways from Califonia and she had no money to get there. We packed our few things and left anyways. I heard her ask at each stagecoach stop 'Just me and my son overnight. Can you break a large denomination gold coin?' No one ever could so we stayed at inns along the way for free. Ma died soon after reaching Cambridge. She hardly ate as we traveled but she made sure there was food for me. I place this note and coin at her grave. I erned the coin mysef and am giving to her what she never had. Lester."

Tears were in Kate's eyes. Lloyd said "I'll take the coin to the pawn shop to learn its value."

Later, Tyler's father hugged him, saying "The value of the coin will pay for a year's college for you. And a few special gifts, too. What a Christmas we will have! And Tyler, I've learned a lesson. From now on, I'll be a better listener. I want you to feel free to tell me anything. I'm very sorry, son."

THE KID AND THE GIFT

As vice-president of Jackson Industries, I've dealt with hundreds of employees over the years and not one got under my skin—until last May, when "the kid" appeared in my office.

She looked to be about 19 or 20 years old and was hired by Human Resources to assist Maggie, my secretary. I was dumbfounded that she passed the first interview. Her blondish hair was unevenly cut and the ends were black, as if she had leaned over a bucket of tar. Her enthusiasm for black eye shadow was the focus of many jokes in the executive lunchroom. "Hey, William," someone would call to me. "Is the EEOC making you hire raccoons now?"

Her name was Amy, but I silently referred to her as "the kid." When Maggie would ask her to fax a report or take a file down the hall, she hobbled precariously atop shoes that must have been Herman Munster's. Although Human Resources assured me that the kid possessed an associate's degree, I had doubts. For example: Wills Creek runs along the south side of our building. Its average depth is probably four or five inches. On some days, you could walk across the creek without getting your ankles wet. One day the kid said she ate her lunch under a tree by the "river." Right, kid, and Salt Fork Lake is an ocean!

My first significant encounter with the kid occurred on Christmas Eve. I let Maggie have the day off to be with her family. I must admit, the kid did a fairly good job by herself that day. Everything was smooth as cream until a thought struck me like a one-ton truck. I needed a Christmas present for my wife! Every year I would get Gloria an expensive piece of jewelry and an article of clothing. For this Christmas I bought her a sparkling emerald and diamond bracelet that matched the necklace I had bought the year before. But I totally forgot about the other present, and it was 2:00 p.m. Christmas Eve.

"Amy, come to my office, please," I called. Clop, clop, clop, echoed the Munster shoes.

"Yes, sir?"

"I need a really big favor. I want you to go to Bloomingdale's at the Byesville Mall and pick a gift for my wife. I usually get her a sweater or a chenille bathrobe."

The raccoon eyes stared blankly at me. "Chenille—is that like terry cloth?"

Please, God, I prayed. *Just get me through this.*

I pushed the money into her hand and said with a touch of impatience, "Just get her something you think a 50-year-old woman would enjoy wearing."

The blank eyes brightened with understanding. "Gotcha!" she said, turning toward the door.

Christmas morning: Gloria was about to open the gift. Bloomingdale's had done a fine job with the wrapping. Candy canes covered the glittering white paper and the tag read: "To My Darling Wife." At that moment I felt proud of the kid.

"I spent a lot of time choosing this for you," I said. What a master I was with the white lie!

Gloria peeled the paper and ribbons from the box and opened it. Her eyes widened and her mouth dropped as she held up the garment to eye level. My mouth dropped also, and my heart nearly jumped out of my chest. The kid had purchased a bubble-gum pink negligee with a white lace bodice, as sheer as a dragonfly's wing. I had seen something like it only once before, and that was 25 years ago at my brother's bachelor party. And the woman wearing it was inflatable.

Tuesday morning I'll march into Human Resources, I said to myself, *and demand the kid's firing. I will personally escort her out the door, and perhaps throw her into the "river!"*

Still holding the monstrosity, Gloria looked at me. Here it comes, I thought.

"Oh, Will," she said, with tears forming. "After all these years, you still think I'm sexy!" She then plopped into my lap and planted a kiss on my cheek. "This is the best Christmas present ever!" she gushed.

"I—I thought you would like it," I stammered.

I still intend to go to Human Resources. That brilliant kid deserves a raise!

LINDA WARRICK

A SIXTIES YULETIDE

December of 1963 was especially cold and gray. The children watched with anticipation as the snow fell soft and thick, quickly coating the trees along the banks of Wills Creek. With any luck, there would be enough snow, as predicted, so their Christmas vacation from school would start a few days early.

It had been four years since Grandpa's passing. Grandma had arrived last night from the farm to spend the holidays with them. Leann, her brother, and her younger sisters loved it when she came to stay for a visit. Even though their little house was crowded and it meant doubling up, it was fun. They loved to hear her stories of the "Old Country," Slovakia. In turn, she was always attentive and listened to their childhood cares and concerns.

Best of all, Grandma was the greatest cook and baker anyone could ever ask for. Everyone looked forward to "helping" her. The children were usually rewarded by getting to lick the mixing spoons before they went in the wash. Helping shell the pecans and chop them for her nut rolls allowed time to work alongside her and listen while she talked.

The children got their wish. By morning, the snow was so deep and the wind so swift that it had whipped the glistening powder into three- and four-foot drifts. Roads were impassable. Sled riding didn't last long, with the wind chill temperatures freezing fingers and toes to dangerous frostbite levels.

Sometime the week before Christmas, Dad would bring back the most perfectly symmetrical fir tree he could find while out on one of his coon hunting expeditions. They couldn't wait to drag out the decorations. The special smell of pine seemed to permeate those treasures stored away and used but once a year.

Out came the strands of great big lights in multicolors. Then the glass ornaments in a variety of silver shapes and colored glitter accents. New ones were never even considered because it wouldn't have been Christmas without the traditional family ornaments.

The finishing touch, of course, was the silver strands of tinsel hung carefully from each bough. These became known fire hazards when coming in contact with the hot lights.

In the mid-60's, the family replaced the live pine with its dropping needles for the new trend in aluminum trees, complete with an ever-changing color wheel. All were mystified by its dazzling sparkle, creating a coziness that would never be forgotten.

Beneath it was the wood and ceramic Nativity scene, swaddled amongst the folds of a white sheet, simulating snow. Scattered around it were beautifully wrapped packages for relatives, reminding the children of the surprises to come from Santa.

Evenings were spent gathered around the old television to watch "The Christmas Story," "The Night Before Christmas," or a "Bing Crosby Christmas Special," with the light of the holiday tree providing the atmosphere.

The children looked forward to placing the Advent calendar of a glittery snow scene, complete with hovering angels, on the wall. Each day a new door cut into it would be opened to reveal a special message leading up to the holiday celebration. Glittered greeting cards and ornaments reflected the soft lights of the holiday decorations.

On Christmas Eve, the anticipation of placing the Baby Jesus amidst the straw in the manger gave it special meaning. Gathered around the lighted tree, with Grandma present, the Slovak custom of passing the Oplatki wafers was practiced. Portions of them were broken off, spread with honey, and given to loved ones, asking special blessings upon them and asking forgiveness and love.

The children found it hard to sleep on Christmas Eve, with thoughts of the day that lay ahead on their minds. It seemed normal to wake each other in the wee hours of the morning and, with a flashlight, take a sneak peek at the names on the gifts that Santa had left under the tree. If Mom and Dad had only known. They probably did.

DONNA WELLS

CHRISTMAS 2010

It was dark. She was terrified. The snow kept falling, the wind was howling, and the sidewalks were slushy. She was wet, cold, and homesick. There were a lot of people wandering to and fro, but no one bothered to look down and see a little one walking all alone. She was shivering and her teeth were chattering. A man with a long beard, dressed in a red suit, nearly stepped on her.

She longed to be home with her family on this stormy night, curled up in front of the fire. Except where was home? Where was the family? Unable to remember where the house was, she turned corner after corner. All the streets began to look alike. Brightly colored lights were everywhere. How did she get so lost? One minute everyone was playing in the backyard: mother, brothers, and sisters all jumping and running in the snow, trying but failing to make snow angels like the kids in the neighborhood. They were all chasing large snowflakes when she suddenly realized that she was all alone and began to try and find the way back home. Home to that lovely house where there was love and warmth and food, only she didn't know how to get there.

The only things she knew for sure were her name, the names of all her brothers and sisters, and that she way too young to be out here all by herself. But where was everyone and why weren't they out searching for her in her hour of need?

Soon food and shelter became secondary concerns as panic began to take over. *I'm going to die cold, alone, and hungry*, she thought, trudging slowly through the snow covered streets. She was becoming weaker and weaker with each step.

Suddenly, she was swooped up into the air. "There you are, you little fur ball. How in the world did you get out of the yard, and what are you doing this side of Wills Creek? I've been looking for you for hours. Good grief, you're freezing," the man said as he hugged her. He pressed her against his chest and wrapped his coat and scarf around her. Finally, feeling warmer, safer, and happier, she began licking his face. Her puppy breath warmed the icicles that had begun to form on his beard. "We need to get you home where your mother can nurse you and I can sit next to the fire with a cup of Marsha's Christmas eggnog."

The man was so nice. He lived in her house and was apparently the boss of the house sometimes, although often the lady seemed to be the one in charge. They both had many names, sometimes they were called Honey, Sweetheart, Dad, Mom, Dear, Darling, John, or Marsha. Whatever their names, Cocoa loved them both.

Cocoa snuggled closer as the man spoke. His deep voice was so soothing. As they hurried home, the man cuddled the tiny brown lab and told the puppy of the wonderful eggnog that Marsha would be preparing. "First, in a large bowl, Marsha will beat 12 egg yolks with sugar until they are pale and thick. Then she will add a pint of bourbon and a cup of brandy. She will stir this mixture well and add in a pint of whipping cream and a quart of half-and-half and beat that at a medium speed with an electric mixer. When the egg whites are beaten until they are stiff, Marsha will fold them into the egg mixture. After refrigerating for at least 30 minutes, she will float a pint of softened vanilla ice cream on top and finish it all off with some freshly grated nutmeg."

"We're almost home Cocoa," the man said with a smile. "The rest of the litter has already been spoken for, but I think you better stay with me and Marsha. That way we can keep a closer eye on you."

JERRY WOLFROM

AN ANGEL TO THE RESCUE

Tug Klinger, covered with snow, stumbled through the door of the Wills Creek Tavern in East Cambridge. "Don't gimme no Merry Christmas," he mumbled. "Gimme a shot of cheap whiskey and a warm Busch."

"Where ya been, Tug?" one of the barflies asked.

"Don't know and don't care."

The bartender glanced at Tug. "You got a pretty good load on, fella."

"Betch yer life, I do. An' it'll get worse before it gets better." Tug grinned through what few teeth he had left. "What time you gonna lock up?"

"Closing early. About nine," the bartender said. "It's Christmas Eve."

Tug squinted at the string of colored lights above the bar. "Them lights is all the Christmas I need. Hit me again."

"You know, Tug, they're having a special Christmas concert over at the Methodist church..."

"Ha!" Tug shot back. "Ain't been inside a church in forty years and I ain't going near one now."

"Let me at least drive you home."

Tug paused. "Sometimes I don't breathe too good in cold weather." With that, he made his way unsteadily to the door. "Happy new year," he croaked, staggering out into the face of the driving snow.

He lived near the beautifully lighted Methodist church. In passing, he caught the strains of Christmas music coming from inside. Tug plodded painfully through the heavy snow until increasing numbness in his legs sent him toppling facedown into the snow. His alcohol-impaired senses partially masked the pain shooting down his left arm.

Regaining his footing, he labored on. The Christmas carols were louder now. Wet and shivering, Tug wanted to find his way into the church vestibule to warm up. But the ice under the snow was treacherous, causing him to tumble again at the church door.

"Oh, my gosh," someone gasped. "It's Tug Klinger. Drunk again."

Through blurry eyes, Tug saw a man and woman standing over him before he blacked out. They carried him inside, where the big register was blowing warm air.

"He's more than drunk," the man said frantically. "It's a heart attack. Get some help!"

The singing suddenly stopped in the sanctuary and dozens of worshipers made their way to the vestibule. "Sing me a Christmas song," Tug mumbled. "My chest hurts. I wanna hear Silent Night."

"We're calling 9-1-1, then we'll sing," the choir director promised.

"Are you an angel?" Tug slurred.

"No, I'm just someone who loves you very much, Mr. Klinger," she replied.

Managing a weak, crooked semiconscious grin, Tug said, "No, I know you're an angel."

As the emergency squad strapped him on a gurney, ten choir members softly sang, "Silent night, holy night...all is calm...all is bright..." Tug managed a tiny wave as he was placed in the ambulance. In the emergency room, he didn't hear the cardiologist whisper to a nurse, "This is bad."

The medical staff was surprised when Tug opened his eyes to mumble, "Silent night...holy night...an angel is looking after me..."

He awoke on Christmas morning, asking for water. With a weak smile, he said, "I need to see the angel. The one from the church."

The nurse summoned another nurse and a doctor who said, "Just take it easy."

"But the angel...saved my life…" Tug protested.

"Of course. There are angels all around us," a nurse said patronizingly, shrugging to the others.

Tug fell back on his pillow. "You don't believe me, but a Christmas angel visited me last night. It made me stronger." With that, he pulled up his sleeve to reveal clearly the outline of an angel on his forearm. The medical team exchanged puzzled glances.

Two weeks later, Tug walked confidently down the aisle of the church to receive heartfelt hugs from the entire choir. "I'll be here every Sunday," he promised, looking directly at Pastor Morris Sturman.

And he was.

DAVE ADAIR

CHRISTMAS EVE 1929

It was Christmas Eve 1929 and the Trail Run Mine had been shut down for two weeks, so Father had no pay. We already owed the Wills Creek company store money and Father refused to borrow any more. But we had plenty of coal to keep our three-room house warm.

I remember that evening a neighbor lady gave Mother a small jar of coal oil for our lamp so we could see to eat our chicken dinner. I guess we were poor, but I did not know it then.

As I lay in bed that night, clutching a wooden fish Father had carved and given me, I looked out of our window at the brightest star in the sky and remember saying aloud, "Happy birthday, Jesus," and, you know, all was well in the world.

Sam Besket

Russell H. Booth, Jr.

Linda Burris

Marilyn Durr

Joy L. Wilbert Erskine

Evelyn Hileman

By Way of Introduction...

Sam Besket is enjoying retirement through a new interest—writing. He writes on current events, crime, and humor, and is a guest columnist in *The Daily Jeffersonian*. An avid reader of history, he lists Dale Brown, Tom Clancy, and Glenn Beck as his favorite authors.

Russell H. Booth, Jr. is the author of books entitled <u>A Brief History of Guernsey County</u> and <u>The Tuscarawas Valley in Indian Days</u>. He shares his interests in history and writing with his son, Rick, a member of CWW, with whom he crafted this book's foreword.

Linda Burris enjoys writing poems and short stories. She contributed stories for CWW's last two books. Her next project is a children's book of Bible stories. Linda enjoys reading many different kinds of books. Her favorites are fiction books about sports, the Amish, law, and medicine.

Marilyn Durr works in both fiction and non-fiction. Her columns have appeared in *The Daily Jeffersonian*. Marilyn's short story, "The Keeper of Toy Soldiers," received honorable mention from the Hamilton Writers Guild. She is currently working on a mystery novel.

Joy L. Wilbert Erskine believes that all media can be clean and wholesome and still tell an engaging story. Her favorite authors are Gerald N. Lund, Stephen E. Robinson, and David Wroblewski. Joy writes poems and short stories, is a guest columnist for *The Daily Jeffersonian*, and has a children's fantasy book in the works.

Evelyn Hileman has been an avid reader since she learned to read. She found out early in life that the entire world opens up to a person who reads. Her adult reading includes biographies, autobiographies, and history. Writing fiction is new to her. She has written a children's book not yet published.

Beverly Justice

Barbara Kernodle-Allen

Beverly Wencek Kerr

Dona McConnell

Dick Metheney

Carey Mozena

Beverly Justice enjoys writing personal essays, poems, and short stories. She cites Henry David Thoreau as one of the greatest influences in her life. Her favorite contemporary writers are Dean Koontz, Stephen King, and Mitch Albom. She shares her home with six cats, who provide endless inspiration.

Barbara Kernodle-Allen has varied reading interests, including history, humor, mystery, fiction, and non-fiction. Currently working on a story of revenge, murder, and conspiracy, she enjoys writing about people, animals, relationships, and descriptions of beauty in ordinary things.

Beverly Wencek Kerr enjoys reading and writing about the places she has visited in her travels. She writes short stories that young and old can enjoy in the Wills Creek series, many based on life experience. Currently, she writes of her travels on her internet blog, *Gypsy Road Trip*.

Dona McConnell is a former corporate writer who now writes fiction. She has contributed short stories to four books and has taught composition at three colleges. Currently, she is working on two books.

Dick Metheney was born in Wadsworth, Ohio, and has lived most of his life in northern Ohio. He moved to Guernsey County when he retired in 2001. Dick has published one book, If It Is God's Will, and has another partially completed. He is a member of the Cambridge Writers Workshop.

Carey Mozena has been writing for years. She started out with poetry and has won a few poetry contests. She has published a novel, The Prince of Two Worlds, and a series of true short stories called *Miracles*.

Harriette Orr

Pam Ritchey

Joetta Varanasi

Linda Warrick

Donna Wells

Jerry Wolfrom

Harriette Orr is a lifelong resident of Guernsey County. She and her husband, Dave, live in the Fairdale area. Mother of three and stepmother of four, now retired from Champion Spark Plug, Harriette enjoys writing family stories, singing with The Cambridge Singers, gardening, quilting, knitting, and antiques.

Pam Ritchey's published works range from poetry and short stories to non-fiction medical articles. She has also authored a young reader's chapter book. Pam was compiler and technical advisor for our first book and does freelance writing, editing, graphic design, and publishing.

Joetta Varanasi developed an early interest in writing when a poem she wrote was published in the Yorkville Hill School newspaper. Her writing interests include poetry, fiction, flash fiction, and life experiences. Rob Hopcott's *A Green Car for Christmas* Christmas letter is among her favorite reading.

Linda Warrick enjoys writing on a variety of topics including human interest stories and life experiences as well as contributing a genealogy column to *The Daily Jeffersonian*. Her other interests include travel, home and garden decor and design, natural healing, and the paranormal.

Donna Wells is a charter member of CWW with a variety of writing and reading interests. Most of her spare time is spent pursuing those interests. She carries a book and a notebook in her car at all times.

Jerry Wolfrom, CWW coordinator, has been writing for more than 50 years. He prefers to write humor, mysteries, and travel articles. He lists John Grisham, Patricia Cornwell, and Randy Wayne White as his favorite authors.

www.ingramcontent.com/pod-product-compliance
Lightning Source LLC
Chambersburg PA
CBHW071323130626
46556CB00004B/1724

* 9 7 8 0 6 1 5 4 0 7 5 2 4 *